MW00638573

THE FLAT WATER RISES

THE
FLAT
WATER
RISES

AN ANTHOLOGY OF SHORT FICTION
BY EMERGING NEBRASKA WRITERS

EDITED BY KYARA BROWN, TANA BUOY, SEAN DUNN, STEPHANIE HEMPEL,

TAYLOR KOCH, STEPHANIE A. MARCELLUS, ERIKA SCHWARTZ, AND LIZ ZISKA

Copyright © 2018
The Flat Water Rises: An Anthology of Short Fiction
by Emerging Nebraska Writers

All rights reserved.

ISBN: 978-1-7320275-2-7

Published by WSC Press

Cover design by Sharon Cole
Layout design by Chad Christensen

Edited by Kyara Brown, Tana Buoy, Sean Dunn, Stephanie Hempel,
Taylor Koch, Stephanie A. Marcellus, Erika Schwartz, and Liz Ziska

WSC Press
1111 Main St.
Wayne, Ne 68787
wscpress.com

CONTENTS

FOREWORD

I STARTED TEACHING CREATIVE WRITING at the University of Nebraska Lincoln in the early 90s. Since then, I've learned a great deal from my students, quite possibly more than I taught them. Be that as it may, one of the lessons I learned early and have tried to impart to all my students is one about the importance of community. "Look around you," I often say on the day we first gather as a group, "look at the people you are with today. These are the people who will be with you the rest of your writing life. They will be the ones who help you learn to write now, who will someday work for magazines or start presses, who may well be the ones who publish your work." What I hope to impress upon them is the idea that we are all in this together and we need to help and nurture the writers around us even as we do the writer within us. "A rising tide lifts all boats," I say.

Evidence of this kind of community building can be found in this so aptly named anthology: *Flat Water Rises*. Many of the writers featured in this collection graduated from the same Nebraska colleges. Many are members of local writing groups where they meet regularly to talk about one another's work, or simply cheer one another on. Their faces, if not already familiar to one another, will become so as the faces in the crowds at readings, conferences, and book release parties. They are building, and joining, the network that buoys them all.

In reading the work of these 22 emerging Nebraska writers, I found myself looking for the one thing that would mark them as Nebraska writers. I admit that the most solid mark I found was in the author biographies at the end. These are working writers who live in *Nebraska*. More importantly, I found in reading their work that they are writers who are interested in the lives around them, who aren't afraid to explore the underbelly of humanity, but are just as willing to see the good in others, who have a knack for what the late poet Bill Kloefkorn used to call "getting just the right words in just the right order."

In this anthology are stories filled with the heartache of living in this modern age. In many of the stories the characters exhibit that emotional restraint so typical of people of this state, a restraint that creates and magnifies the inherent loneliness of human beings anywhere, not simply in Nebraska. Here are stories told with plain language so clear it hurts to look at the images evoked; stories told with poetic prose so lilting it bears re-reading sentence by sentence; stories told through metaphors that turned slight details into epics. These stories are not simply evocations of place, but evocations of people, of humanity. I came away from reading this collection believing that these writers aren't writing simply *from* the geographical heart of the country, but, to borrow William Gass's words, they are writing *about* the heart of the heart of the country.

—Karen Gettert Shoemaker, author of *The Meaning of Names*

THE FLAT WATER RISES

The Grace of Time

I TAP MY FEET RAPIDLY against the cement floor as my eyes linger on the clock attached to a pillar at the entrance of the train station. I am seated on a bench by the railway platform, listening to the endless ticking of the clock and wringing my backpack straps with my hands. I have not seen Grace in a few days. The thought of being in her presence again makes my stomach twist into a knot; I am not sure if that's a good feeling or a bad one. This only reinforces the tapping. The distant horn of the train catches my attention. I stand up as the train screeches to a stop. The gust of wind that the train brings slaps my face furiously, and that's when I hear it. It's weak, but prominent.

"Time is of essence. Waste none of it," says the wind as Grace steps off the train, her demeanor delicate but firm.

I watch her wearily, the hairs on the nape of my neck raised by the urgency with which the words are spoken. One look at Grace, though, and I forget about my worries. A soft breeze brushes through her honey hair like fingers kneading dough. Her curls bounce as she walks towards me, her lovely spring dress wrapping around her legs like water, and her steps graceful yet careful. I notice that she isn't wearing her favorite white shoes. In fact, she isn't wearing any shoes at all.

As Grace gets closer, I notice a slight black line over her chest. Splashes of vibrant rosy and emerald colors decorate her cleavage, just beyond the black line.

"Hey, Grace. You look beautiful today," I say timidly.

Grace's green eyes crinkle, her nose scrunches ever so slightly at the tilt of her smile. "What is this? Are you being shy?"

I feel my face heat up. "I'm just being honest." I offer my arm to my beloved. She wraps both her hands around my bicep. Her chest rises and falls with eagerness, the black line finally taking shape before my eyes; a butterfly, large and majestic, spreading its wings from her collarbones to her shoulders. "Wanna go to the beach today?"

I know the answer before Grace smiles her consent. I sling my backpack over my shoulder, and we exit the train station. The noise of early morning greets us: cars honk as they proceed to their destinations, lines of people wait in front of food trucks while the cooks shout orders, children shriek with joy as they hang from the monkey bars of a nearby park. My eyes glimpse the park's empty set of swings. I remember a few years ago when Grace declared swings an essential part of a park. Aside from airplanes, she'd said swings were the closest thing humans had to experiencing flight. One could swing higher and higher until they almost touched the sky. I smile fondly at the memory.

A small tug on my arm snaps me out of my reverie. I turn around to find Grace alarmingly close to the street. She does not react to the cars but only stares at them absentmindedly. The drivers, on the other hand, don't appear to pay her any mind. They continue to drive without slowing down.

I resist the urge to snatch her away.

"Love, what are you doing?" I say softly, though I feel my heart pulsing in my throat.

Grace directs her attention to me after a second's hesitation, her lips spreading into a smile. "Nothing. Just thinking."

I try to stop the shakiness of my hands and grin instead. I gently tug Grace away from the street and move to the trail that leads away from the city. The trail is evenly paved, the concrete slightly gray with the hundreds of steps that have walked on it. I know that at the end of the trail lies a town, though I have never been to it. I smell the faint aroma of salt that lingers in the breeze. Soon, the tall buildings and stained-glass windows fade away and are replaced by green forest. We walk in comfortable silence, enjoying the birds' morning songs, the cantor of the cicadas, and a faraway melody that is carried by the wind. My sandals strike the concrete path rather loudly, but Grace's steps are close to nonexistent. I bet if the whole forest became silent, I still wouldn't hear Grace's steps.

I decide to ask her the question I've kept to myself since she stepped off the train. "Grace, where are your shoes?"

She ponders, her free hand under chin and her eyes squinted in thought. "I lost them somewhere."

Suddenly the trail unwinds, and we arrive at the town. The air smells of fried patties and aloe ointments. People stroll down the narrow streets, basking in the abundance of pastel-colored homes and delighting in the smells of each shop. Farther down the road, a path strays to the west. It is there that the port stands, its long planks leading to the three fishing boats anchored to the shore. Grace leads us to as many boutiques and shops as our feet will carry us. I don't mind the detour. She looks so happy wandering from antique store to food vendor that we do as she pleases. A store owner gifts me a single flower, a red amaryllis, which I use to pin Grace's hair behind her ear.

The owner's expression softens when he looks at Grace. His mouth slants, his eyes bright with an emotion so intense that I feel uneasy. His are knowing eyes and that only unsettles me further. I gently pull Grace away to another shop. There we buy fresh coconuts, their shells cold like Grace's hands. We stick a straw in one of the holes at the top and drink from it as we continue our trek to the beach. A few other people give us the same passionate looks, their brows raised in anticipation as if they have witnessed such a scene before. I am about to say something, anything to divert their stares, but Grace squeezes my hand and all the tension leaves my body.

After passing by a grove of palm trees, we reach the beach. At this time the sun has locked directly over our heads. The water sparkles and sand glistens, its smooth surface the only indicator of its total vacancy. I take off my sandals and carry them with my free hand. The sand feels pleasantly warm. Grace's bare feet leave no print on the sand, nothing to announce her arrival to this sunny, wonderful day. She always was very lightweight; still, my pulse accelerates ever so slightly. I interlace my fingers with her. My shadow follows suit, but I am baffled to find the space next to me, where Grace's should be, empty. My shadow holds onto empty, barren space.

"Hey love, where is your shadow?" I ask.

Grace absentmindedly eyes the sand. "It must have run off somewhere."

"Don't worry, I'll fetch it."

I don't wait for Grace to answer me. I whistle loudly. It takes a few moments before my shadow elongates in the sand, its dark outline suddenly detaching from the ground and hovering before me.

"Find Grace's shadow, will you, dear?"

The shadow is gone in a blink of an eye.

Grace and I find a perfect place to rest, close enough to the shore to taste the salt of the ocean in the air but far enough so we don't get wet by strong tides. I seek a thick, auburn blanket from my backpack and place it on the ground. Grace settles down on the blanket and stretches her long legs from the rigorous walk, her pale features bright against the afternoon sun. I want to join her, but the feeling of weariness has returned. Instead, I take off my clothing and hesitantly dip my feet in the cool water. I shiver, but it doesn't take long before I adjust to its temperature.

Then I walk further into the sea, the algae slithering past my legs, until the water reaches my thighs.

"Grace, come to the water! It's absolutely lovely," I shout over the crash of the waves on the shore.

Grace watches me as I tread deeper in the water. She shakes her head and flashes her perfect array of white teeth into a grin. I briefly smile before succumbing to the temptation of the sea. I clutch my knees and sink to the bottom. The sand rubs roughly against my bottom, the current gently pushing me deeper into the sea. My long, dark hair floats around me like seaweed, which I guess is the reason why a swarm of fish suddenly comes into view.

The fish circle around my hair, some of them brave enough to peck at it with their plump lips. The faint sun illuminates their bright shades of coral, turquoise, and lavender, their eyes focused on nothing but my hair. That is, with the exception of one fish. This one is bigger than the others, stout and lilac, its eyes glazed over with blindness. It floats before me, though it wobbles from time to time. It looks at me with its distant glare.

"Beware." Its deep and scratchy voice alarms me, but I don't let it show. "Time is almost over."

The old fish swims back to its colleagues, blending in with their flash of color. Soon they grow bored of my hair and swim away back into the deep, blue sea. I jump back to the surface, letting the last of my breath out in an explosion of bubbles that circles around my body. The current has definitely risen during my absence. The blanket is a darker shade from its dampness, the edges speckled with wet sand. Grace sits exactly where I left her, dry and happy. Somehow, seeing her smile like that doesn't make me any less uneasy.

The sun now lies closer to the west, the sky tinted with oranges, pinks, and blues. Grace procures a towel from my backpack and hands it to me.

"We should probably hang the towel to dry."

Grace holds my hand and pulls me down next to her. "It doesn't bother me. I barely feel it."

I wrap an arm around her shoulder, my eyes fixed on the vastness of the sea before me. We sit like that for a long time, Grace's head leaning against my shoulder, our breathing even, and the sun slowly following its trajectory west. The silence begins to clench my heart. The sky keeps darkening, a splurge of indigo coming to view.

"Do you want to find a place to stay for the night?"

"Oh, but why would we do that? I love the night sky," says Grace with a hint of surprise in her tone.

I stay quiet and swallow my increasing dread. The sun is reaching the horizon when there is a movement at the corner of my eye. Both Grace and I turn to see my shadow looming over us.

"Did you find it?" I say.

The shadow responds by drifting away to the grove of palm trees that lies a few feet away from us.

Grace and I exchange glances before following the frantic shadow. We weave through the groves until they become a forest, the air suddenly heavy with humidity. From time to time the shadow blends in with patches of darkness as the sun continues to set. The shadow stops in front of a palm tree, though I don't see the difference between this one and the rest of the forest. Then I look up and my heart sinks. A pair of white shoes hangs from a branch, swaying gently to the breeze.

I look at Grace. Her expression mirrors those of the townsfolk, her eyes sad and her smile smaller than it's been all day. The butterfly on her chest moves up and down, as if getting ready to take flight.

"I guess that's where my shoes went," says Grace, her voice barely more than a whisper. "Can you fetch them for me, love?"

How can I say no when she speaks so softly like that, when her frame becomes more fragile with the burden of her words? My shadow returns to me as I stretch my arms and legs, reaching for anything to keep me steady as I climb and climb. My mind races desperately for a sign to help me escape this fate. My limbs feel numb from the exertion. The shoes dangle calmly, their whiteness marked by the colors of the sunset. I grab the shoes and descend smoothly back to the muddy ground.

There is a moment of stillness when Grace and I stare at each other, Grace's eyes wide with anticipation, mine hard with regret. She holds her hands out. I give her the shoes. Everything about this action is so easy, yet so difficult. Time has indeed run out, and I'd been a fool to believe this moment could last forever. Without needing guidance from my shadow, we return to the beach. My feet know where to go. The sun is now halfway through the horizon, the sky tainted with purples and indigo. A few stars twinkle in the distance.

Grace slip on the shoes. A sigh of relief escapes her thin lips. "Ah yes, now I remember."

Sorrow tugs at my heart. I pull Grace into an embrace, my eyes stinging with the familiar burn of tears. Grace returns the hug, patting my back ever so gently and cooing soft words into my ears.

"You know that I love you, right?" I say through the thickness of sadness. Grace nods.

"You know I'm going to miss you."

"I know."

I pull away, taking in the image of Grace's little nose, the sharpness of her cheekbones and the silkiness of her skin. I hold her hand tightly. "I will never forgive you for leaving me like this. Never."

Grace chuckles softly. She takes my face in her small hands and kisses my forehead. "Oh, love. You already have."

Only a sliver of the sun remains over the horizon. The butterfly on her chest swells and comes to life in a burst of color. Not one butterfly, but many, all of them stemming from every limb of Grace's body. Her dress, her legs, her stomach, her flesh, turn to butterflies of crimson, aqua, rose, teal, and violet. They fly upwards, fading with the glare of the sun. I hold onto Grace until her hands disappear. From her lips, she utters "Farewell" before her face vanishes with the flutter of wings.

I lie down on the wet blanket, my eyes exhausted from shedding tears. I watch as day becomes night, the black sky speckled with an infinite amount of stars reflecting off the resting sea. The wind chills my skin, but I find it refreshing against the numbness of my limbs. Her last word echoes in my ears. The moon illuminates my footsteps on the sand, a solemn reminder of her eternal absence.

Notice

THE DEFROST HAD FINALLY STARTED working on the windows. Drips of water ran down the windshield, making it look as if it were raining. The inside was warming up, seat heaters making the black leather almost too hot. NPR radio played in the background, soothing in its monotonous drone. The ever-present scent of Black Ice air freshener was stronger than normal, a newly opened cardboard tree flapping in the blow of the heater. Andrea loved this car as much as she loved the man it belonged to, and the familiarity was a comforting presence. Jackson flipped on the windshield wipers, dispersing the rest of the moisture from the glass, allowing both of them to clearly view the grand colonial style mansion already lit for Christmas. If she didn't know any better, she would think that the family who lived in the house were warm and inviting.

"Listen, if I knew my grandfather and his wife were going to be here, I would never have brought you," Jackson told her while playing with the temperature settings. "I'm just so embarrassed. Can you forgive me?" he questioned, finally looking her in the eye.

She thought about his question and thought about the last two hours she had spent in the rolling mansion. Jackson's grandfather had been lounging in the formal sitting room, crystal tumbler filled with two fingers of scotch, grasped lazily in his hand. He immediately embraced his favorite grandson, enfolding him in his ample stomach. His Princeton class ring caught the light of the chandelier as he thumped Jackson heartily on the back. The joyful welcome was quickly over when Grandpa Simon glimpsed Andrea in the entryway. Joy turned to question and then almost immediately into disapproval as his green eyes took her in.

She had made sure that her outfit was appropriate for the occasion, wanting to make a good impression on their first Thanksgiving together. Her favorite deep purple blouse went well with her skin and made her feel confident and powerful. She wore it the day she interviewed at her financial firm. She bought a pair of black cigarette pants two days ago to go with it, and her natural curls were tamed in a tasteful top bun. The small diamond earrings Jackson gave her for her birthday shined prettily in her ears. Grandpa Simon's look made her feel like she was a beggar on the street.

"It was an experience," she finally answered impartially, running her hand agitatedly against her leg. Grandpa Simon had made numerous references to the "savior" of the country, their current president, and every time he mentioned the "silent majority" his wife of four months looked pointedly at Andrea. Jackson's mother tried her best to keep a Stepford-wife smile plastered on her mouth, but Andrea could see it fall ever so slightly anytime it was aimed in her direction. Jackson's father's apple didn't fall far from the tree, but instead of making pointed remarks about politics like his father, Grandpa Simon, he chose to ignore her the entire time they were there. She found it slightly annoying that Jackson only noticed the obvious.

"Honestly, I should apologize for my family as well," she sighed, squinting out the window on her side, trying to make out the neighboring houses though she could barely see that far away. "I never expected that from them."

"What are you talking about?" asked Jackson, taking out his frustrations at his family by running his hand through his blond hair almost violently. "They were great."

She scoffed looking over at his green eyes, so much like those of the men that raised him, shaped some of who he was, but instead of hate they glistened with adoration. She memorized that look. She guessed he might not have noticed that her Uncle Ronnie had stopped telling his favorite joke as soon as he remembered that Jackson was in the room. It involved a white guy as the punchline. Big belly, so much like Grandpa Simon's, bouncing with mirth and then suddenly still. His good shirt was the only one that still buttoned over his growing girth, and Andrea noticed even that one was straining. Silver sprinkled his black hair salt and pepper, and she knew he was keeping his fade cut a little lower because he was going bald. Her great-grandmother kept calling Jackson "boy" in some snub that didn't quite make sense to Andrea other than she knew it was rude, and her grandmother asked him repeatedly if he had been to any "meetings" lately. The fact that he didn't notice any of that and seemed to have a great time with her family annoyed her too.

"Listen we've been together almost a year now, and you just made junior partner at the financial firm. We just survived coming back home to this rinky-dink town from the Big Apple and each other's families. I think we can count this as a win," he stated, grabbing her hand and squeezing it tight. His smile made her sad, but she memorized it too.

"I guess," she mumbled, staring at their fingers intertwined.

Their hands lay on the gear shift. Colors swirled together. His gripped hers tight, nails almost white with pressure, secure like it always was. Hers was soft and slightly cold despite the warmth in the car, hold a little looser than normal. He didn't notice.

KYARA BROWN
Woman

IT WAS THE SIGHT OF THE BLOOD that made her steel herself against the emotions. She looked at the bright spots blemishing the white cotton she thought she was safe in wearing, cursing herself for feeling anything in the first place. If she had ignored her baser self, her weaker self, there would be no emotion to cordon off. She had let herself drift, however, sink into the happiness as it lapped against her skin. She had luxuriated in the glow, warming herself in the rays, cat-like in her superiority. This is what she got for being so stupid. She stared harder at the spots of shame, willing them to go away, but there was no disappearing the truth.

She glanced at the door to the bathroom. She could hear the noise of the party just beyond the door, leaking joy and expectation under the slim crack between the soft carpet of the hallway and the cold tile of the bathroom. The gathering was supposed to be the first of many just like it, friends and family all together to celebrate new lines on pages she had started writing from the time she was a little girl: wife, master business woman, mother. Chapters had already been composed: married to a wonderful man at twenty-five, rising star at her PR firm not six months later, and this was supposed to be the starting sentence to the most important ink in the story of her life. She couldn't believe this could be happening to her again.

She had thought they were safe this time, eight weeks in, much longer than the five times before. She organized the party to announce it to the most important people in her life, not a lot of people, just the ones she loved the most. A quick flash of her husband's devastated face stabilized in her mind. It would only be a second, maybe two, the deep lines on his forehead between his eyes would appear, more tight and serious than normal. His eyes would glaze over, and she knew he would be picturing all of the future events he had let himself hope for birth, middle of the night feedings, petty arguments over who would change the diaper, first day of school, first date, graduations, marriage, grandchild being placed in his arms, all gone, again. He would fix his face though, he always did. He would look her in her eye and tell her that they would try again, that next time would be the time that their deepest wish finally came true.

A quiet sob escaped her before she could choke it down, bitter and rotten. She had to get herself together; she had to find her husband and let him know that an announcement would have to wait. She kept herself seated though, letting herself feel nothing, think nothing more. A burst of laughter sometime later woke her from her quiet. She got a pad from under the sink and a fresh pair of underwear, black this time, from the clean clothes pile in the corner of the bathroom.

She prepared to go out into the crowd and the happy atmosphere she would have to pretend she wanted to be a part of. Standing in front of the mirror, bracing herself against the sink, she slowly looked up into her reflection, the only features of herself she would probably ever see. Breasts, high and slightly swelled. Hips, flared and ready. Features of a woman, features that belonged to a woman, features that should not belong to her.

TANA BUOY

The Playground for Lost Boys

TWO SILHOUETTES JERK. ONE IS OVERLY aggressive in manner while the other simulates equitable movements in an involuntary response set in motion to the lewd performance projecting onto the backdrop of the decaying brickwork of Wu's Hot Pot.

A stench of rotting vegetables and spoiled chicken wafts from the pile of garbage bags, mixing with the rancid smell of something a lot seedier seeping out from between the mortar. Before this place became the Void's hotspot for exquisite cuisine and cheap takeout, it had been a large textile factory—a subtle reminder of the times before child labor laws existed. *Funny*. He wonders if they ever existed at all. If these laws were just some fairytale spun for the unwanted people by the Void's education system.

Ignoring the animalistic grunts in his ear and the forced strain in his neck due to the violent tugs of his hair, Bat forces himself to focus past their shadows and onto the large logo. The hundred-and-some-year-old paint has faded a lot since then, its personalized insignia barely visible under the low-lit gaslight on the side of the building. He wonders what it would have been like working there. Those long grueling hours. Low wages. If it was as bad as—*as what?*

The words *be grateful* are pounded harder into him every time, forming bruises over old bruises over older ones. Forming even now, on his hands and knees, and with pants pushed down past his thighs, he chooses to believe that those laws never existed. Worked to exhaustion, were they tossed from the upper windows—those children—down into this very alleyway? Or did they jump? He imagines this place littered with the broken bodies of useless boys, piled on top of each other in wheelbarrows and hauled off to where? To a resting place, a final peace? Bat can only hope.

§

Bat walks from out of the alley, shoving the bills into the front pocket of his jeans before throwing his tank top back over his head. The man— his client—exits after, casually losing himself in the mix of suit and ties conveniently walking past, no doubt heading over to one of the fancy bars up the block. They are all too busy conversing about tomorrow's stock market to notice the disheveled intruder. Bat loses sight of him as the group rounds the corner. He allows himself to exhale deeply, easing his shoulders back against the cool brick. The street is quiet, void of people for the time being. Eyelids falling, he fingers through the thick dark curls on his head, letting his fingertips massage his sore scalp.

He is instantly aware of the change of air, a huff as another body falls against the wall. Bat's nose scrunches. He doesn't need to see to know who it is. "Dude, you fucking stink."

"Well excuse me, if I don't get to revel in the scent transference of $2,100 Clive Christian. Must be rough." Although the comment is laced in sarcasm, he isn't in the mood for Gandhi's drug-induced humor.

Bat smirks and opens his eyes, stares down at the ground. He is tired. *So tired.* "Think if we ask, we can get Diego to redo the sidewalk?" The pavement is riddled with a series of new cracks, webbing from the larger chunks of missing concrete. "It's already a walking hazard, and soon everyone will find a new route. New curb appeal. Where will that leave us, man?" And to himself, he thinks, *where will that leave me?* It's a double-edged sword that cuts him either way.

The other boy shrugs, "Probably not. Unless you're planning to use your fuck money to pay for it." Gandhi pushes the hood of his oversized jacket back from his oblong, clean-shaven head. "Besides doesn't leave me anywhere I need to worry about. I'm a dealer, not a—" his voice trails off. "Shit, dude," he slurs. "That came out wrong, I'm sorry. Here do you want . . ." Gandhi shoves a bony hand into the large side pocket, pulls out a handful of bags containing a variety of substances. "To make you feel better. Maybe something to make you get off to the next . . ."

"Shut up, Gandhi," Bat snaps as a white Royce slowly drives past and pulls up to the curb a few yards away, an ominous red glow casting onto the street from the brake lights. "Just, shut up." His worn black sneakers with the broken soles thump against the pavement towards the passenger side of the car. In front of the tinted window, he pulls up the bottom of his dark green tank top to not only wipe his face, but to give the driver a glimpse of his muscular torso, shining with sweat in the streetlight. Bat stares at his reflection, a blank void of emotion in his dark eyes, a version of himself he no longer knows, and slowly he watches it disappear, his face replaced with that of his potential client.

The man is an older gentleman, white mustache and balding on the top. He is in some black gym suit get-up. Has a friendly sort of look about him.

"Hey there, sir." He smiles. Winks. "Name's Bat. What can I do you for?"

"How old are you, kid?" the man asks, not looking Bat directly in the eye.

"Eighteen." He was told always go with eighteen, because anything below that could get him in trouble and nineteen could screw him out of money.

He nods, and Bat gives the usual spiel: menu, terms and conditions, extra add-on costs.

The man nods again. "Get in," he says, leaning over and opening the door from the inside. "And be careful," he adds. "I just had this detailed."

Bat notices a large gym towel thrown over the front of the back rest, and another across the seat. A large garbage bag is spread open on the floor—Bat assumes it is for his feet. He makes sure to step onto it before settling back onto the covered seat. In reality, he should be offended, but he isn't. Been doing this way too long to be offended by much of anything.

Bat looks out the side mirror as they drive away. Gandhi is still standing where he left him. The dark hood pulled back over his shaved head, arms crossed against his chest, staring down at a large fissure in the sidewalk— bloodshot eyes watching it widen, waiting to swallow him whole. All he had to do was jump. All any of them had to do was jump.

SOPHIE CLARK
The Jesus Game

AFTER BEDTIME, MY BROTHER AND I played Mary and Joseph.
First, we listened for blankets, the other sliding from their twin bed and onto
their toes. Before we met in our Jack and Jill bathroom, we pulled our shirts
up to our foreheads so that they hung down our backs like headscarves. I was
the one who brought Jesus—my small black baby doll, swaddled in spare
pajamas. My brother pulled the hand towel from its hook and draped it over
the sink stool for a manger. We kneeled beneath our fluorescent ceiling light
and waited. We always waited for the Wise Men first. When they didn't come,
we waited for the Shepherds, listening for hooves. Finally, we whispered for
the Little Drummer Boy. We *ruh-bum-bum-bah*-ed softly until we heard the
first sound coming from across the hall. A fear we could never explain always
sent us quickly pattering for our beds, pulling our shirts back—me, kicking
baby Jesus deep into my blankets.

GUSTAVO CRUZ
Flight Time

I STEPPED OFF THE PLANE and onto the passenger boarding bridge as the flight attendant with the short blonde hair smiled and waved. "Welcome to Fargo. Have an excellent evening, and try to stay warm," she said, the winter wind gusting loudly past the open space between the aircraft and the bridge. I'd flown out of Denver that evening, and I hoped to be in Minneapolis by midnight. Instead, I found myself stranded in Fargo at half past nine due to "extreme weather conditions."

Hector International Airport was the smallest airport I'd ever seen. The arrivals and departures screen listed only five gates, and each one—written in bright red letters—read: FLIGHT CANCELLED. I pulled the strap of my carry-on off my shoulder, letting the old gym bag I'd had since high school drop to the floor. The concourse was so small that I needed only to turn around to see every gate from where I stood. All the gates were closed, and the concourse deserted. I took out my cell phone and contemplated calling my father. My brother, Martín, was being released from prison that Friday, and

I had hoped to spend the weekend with my family in Minneapolis helping Martín settle back into society.

On a nearby wall a television was playing. There was a local weatherman on the screen, but he was like no meteorologist I'd ever seen.

"Too Tall Tom here, and it's coooooollldddd outside, folks!" the weatherman said with a booming voice and a vowel-heavy, almost Canadian-like, accent. "We've got temperatures below the donut this evening. That's right, sub-zero weather!"

Too Tall seemed to assault the television with his forecast, whipping his long arms around the weather map before leaning in so close that his head filled the screen. "Don't believe me? Just follow me," Szymanski said, waving for the cameraman to follow. He grabbed a mug of coffee from offscreen and ducked under an exit sign as he opened the studio doors and stepped into a snowy parking lot. He threw the coffee high into the air, and white vapor filled the sky. The camera panned up, then down, focusing on the brown shards of ice shattered across the blacktop. The camera panned up to Too Tall. "That's how cold it is, and it's going to get a lot worse."

I reached the ground floor of the tiny airport and stuck my phone back in my coat pocket. One employee was still standing at the Delta Airlines desk, and she was busy assuring a red-faced man that he would be on the first flight out of Fargo the next morning.

"My ticket says I'm supposed to be in Chicago tonight. I *expect* to be in Chicago tonight," the middle-aged man said, pointing at his flight itinerary.

The woman never flinched. "I understand that, sir, but I don't control the weather. The best I can do is give you a free stay at a hotel and book you on the next flight out."

The man sighed loudly and balled up his fist as he shook his head side to side. I felt a slight chill at the sight of his furled brow and quivering lip, and I shivered as I realized I'd seen that look before. It was the same look I'd seen on my brother's face countless times during our teenage years.

I hadn't seen Martín since he'd been sentenced to twenty years for attempted murder. It was nothing more than an argument over a parking space, but when the man in the Cadillac called my brother a "stupid spick," Martín didn't stop hitting him until three grown men pulled him off. That was twelve years ago. Martín wasn't an angry, brash twenty-year-old anymore. He was a man who'd earned a college degree and wrote children's books from his prison cell. He was ready to be paroled, and I was eager to welcome him home.

The red-faced man unclenched his fist and accepted the hotel voucher to a nearby Ramada.

"Here you are, Mr. Michael Greer," she said, reading his name off the voucher. "The last shuttle to the Ramada arrives in about ten minutes."

Greer walked away.

"And I suppose you're going to need a voucher and a new flight too," she said, never looking up from her computer.

"Leonardo Rodriguez," I replied. "To Minneapolis."

§

The shuttle dropped us off at the hotel across town, and Greer and I darted across the icy street, bracing against the brutal windchill. We both turned to face the large glass doors after entering. We breathed heavily against the glass and watched the snow fall and swirl back into the air. We both shivered and stomped at the floor mats, shaking the snow from our coats.

Greer and I approached the front desk. We both slid our hotel vouchers toward the young woman. Her name tag read: CELINE.

Celine smiled nervously as she gathered up the vouchers like note cards for a speech she was preparing. "I'll be right back," she said, leaving through an office door.

Moments later, Celine returned with her supervisor.

"My name's Jessie. I'm the hotel manager," the tall man with the slight Northern accent said, shaking our hands politely. "Here's the problem, guys. We're all booked up, and no one's leaving because of the blizzard—"

"Aren't you a hotel?" Greer interjected. "What the hell do we do now?!" his lip quivered with rage.

"Umm...Well, you guys are welcome to wait on the couches in the lobby or—"

Greer raised an open hand in protest. "Wait a minute. The lobby? Are you serious!?" He placed both hands on the desk and leaned forward. "How much are these vouchers worth?"

The manager took a step back and stood up straighter. "You're absolutely right, sir. Our bar usually closes at nine o'clock, but I'm willing to open it back up and honor these vouchers for food and drink purchases if you like."

Greer seemed satisfied with the manager's suggestion, and he relaxed his posture and stepped back from the desk.

Three hours later, he and I had each sampled four shots of the bar's most expensive tequila, shared a chicken quesadilla, and knocked back at least five beers each as we watched ESPN on the bar TVs. Jessie served as bartender, and he gave us each $200 bar tabs.

"So, what kind of name is Leonardo anyway?" asked Greer, with a slight slur in his voice.

Surprised, I turned away from the boxing highlights I had been fixated on and said, "I'm Mexican American. Everyone calls me Lee though. Only my dad calls me Leonardo."

"You're Mexican?" he asked, still slurring. "Really? You don't *look* Mexican."

Jessie was busy washing pint glasses at the sink behind the bar, but he paused to listen in on our conversation as he set the glasses out to dry on a white towel.

I shifted around on my bar stool. I took a sip of my beer, and I collected my thoughts for a moment. Maybe I was influenced by the four shots of tequila, but I simply couldn't help myself. I turned to Greer and asked, "What exactly do Mexicans look like?"

"Okay, let's take it easy, you two," Jessie said, typing numbers into the point of sale touchscreen.

"It's a simple question," I continued. "If he educates me on what Mexicans are supposed to look like, maybe I can educate my Mexican family."

Greer rose from his stool. "You wanta take this outside, boy?" he asked, tossing the stool to the side.

"Hey!" the acting bartender yelled, bringing his palm down hard on the bar. "That's it. You're both cut off!" Jessie reached for our drinks, lifting them off the table and pouring them down the sink drain.

"Alright, I'm done anyway." I stepped off my stool, stumbling a bit as I stood.

Greer reached across the bar for his drink as Jessie poured it out. "You son of a bitch," he said, flailing his arms.

Jessie pulled the glass further from his grasp. "You're done."

Greer pulled a liquor bottle from the bar well and threw it at the hotel manager. The bottle slipped from his hand and struck the television above our heads. Cheap vodka and shards of broken glass showered all around us.

Furious, Jessie walked out from behind the bar. "You're out of here!" he yelled.

Greer raised his fists, took one step back, and slipped on the debris. He fell back hard, banging his head on the tile floor.

I waited on the couch in the lobby and watched as a towering plow cleared away the snowdrifts that had gathered over the preceding hours. The sound of sirens followed, and the Fargo police and paramedics—in their extreme cold weather gear—trudged through the blowing snow and entered the Ramada. While Jessie explained the situation to the police, the paramedics strapped Greer to a board and whisked him away in an ambulance. I took out my cell phone and sent my father a text: "I won't be there on time, but nothing will stop me from arriving."

GUSTAVO CRUZ
Working the Two Train

A SEVENTEEN-YEAR-OLD BOY STOOD, silently looking down the barrel of a three-fifty-seven revolver, while the downtown two train sped along its fixed path. Topher could feel the vibrations of the rumbling car travel from the soles of his shoes, up his torso, and into the depths of his racing heart. He didn't hear the stampede of startled passengers frantically shoving past him and fighting each other for use of car 7657's door. He didn't hear the screaming woman awakened by the blast of gunfire begin hyperventilating— ragged, rapid breaths escaping her cupped hands. Topher didn't feel the blood slowly dripping down his face as he struggled not to let the gunman see his body tremble.

"Your friend doesn't look so good," the gunman said.

Topher didn't reply. The high-powered revolver was intimidating—but Topher could see into the gun's five-chamber cylinder, and by his count— there were only two bullets remaining.

"You look fine to me though," the gunman said, cocking the hammer back and pressing the barrel into the boy's cheek.

Topher closed his eyes and exhaled. He pictured his mother. He knew she was probably sitting at the kitchen table, sipping from a rocks glass of Jack Daniels, as she pored over a stack of past-due bills. He wished he could hug her one last time and smell the odd but familiar mix of cheap, knock-off perfume and Tennessee whiskey.

He opened his eyes. "Maybe if I make a run for it now," he thought, "he'll miss. I'm sure I could outrun him if I make it through the car door."

As Topher planned his escape, looking from the barrel to the cylinder to the door, the gunman smirked and pulled the trigger.

§

Topher Jackson was your average "kid-from-a-broken-home" sob story. He'd lived in New York all his life. He'd never met his father, his mother was a part-time alcoholic/part-time waitress, and his mother and he were constantly on the verge of homelessness.

One evening, Topher and his best friend since kindergarten, Anton, waited for the two train to arrive. It was a Saturday, and the subway station was packed tight with New Yorkers and tourists on their way to Manhattan bars, theaters, and other hotspots.

"Why you in such a mood today?" Anton asked, pointing to the scowl on Topher's face.

Topher sucked his teeth. "Man, my mom got mugged last night."

"What? For real?" Anton shook his head and sighed.

"Yeah. Some junkie took her whole roll at knifepoint, right outside the bank. I don't know how she's gonna pay rent." Topher brought his hands to his forehead, closed his eyes, and massaged his temples. "The damn power company already cut the lights off. It's like we're livin' in a cave."

Anton placed his hand on his friend's shoulder. "Hey, come on now. It's gonna be alright. How much you need?"

Topher scoffed. "How the hell *you* gonna pay *my* rent?"

"I'm not. But I bet we can make enough, right now, to maybe get the lights on."

Topher shifted his weight from side to side. "How?"

"Ain't you never worked the train? It's easy. Start at the last car, and hit every car on your way to the front. Just ask little old ladies and weak, scared-lookin' dudes for a few bucks."

"That works?"

"Open your eyes. People do it every day." Anton gestured to the restless crowd milling about all around them, most of them absently swiping at their iPhones. "They all got money. And, on the train, some of 'em will pay a few bucks just to get us to walk away."

The two train coasted to a stop, and a flood of passengers disembarked. The boys slipped their way through the crowd and boarded the last car. "If somebody doesn't wanta donate, be persuasive," Anton said as Topher and he took their seats at the back. "Give 'em a little attitude. That's why you wanta look for weak, shy people."

"Okay," Topher said, as he scanned the seats and benches for the right person.

Anton pointed, keeping his hand close to his chest and speaking in a whisper. "I'd say the grandma on the bench with the little girl, the executive in the suit yapping into his phone, and the skinny, pale, pasty-lookin' dude in the jacket over at the end."

The passenger doors closed, and the train jolted forward. Anton and Topher walked down the center of the aisle, smiling and nodding. "Hey, ma'am, is it cool if I get five dollars? My buddy's momma got robbed on the street," Anton said to the grandma.

"That's terrible," she said, handing Topher a ten from her purse.

Mr. Executive-on-the-cellphone raised his arm and showed the boys his palm (the universal signal for "just a moment") as he scolded his secretary. "And now I've got panhandlers taking the money right out of my damn wallet on the train," he said, handing the boys a five. "Yeah, you better fix it . . ."

Topher stuffed the bill in his pocket with the ten.

"Hey, buddy. How you doin'?" Anton said to the pasty man, flashing a wide smile.

Pasty remained silent. He seemed to stare right through the boys.

Anton waved his hand in the man's face. "Hey, man. I'm right here. You awake?"

Topher shifted his weight, gesturing toward the car door. "Let's just go, Anton."

"No, no. He can talk. He can say 'no' or 'screw off' or somthin'." Anton sat next to the man. "We're gonna be buddies."

Pasty put his hands in his jacket pockets. "You're not my buddy. What do you want?"

Anton stood and stepped in front of the man (right next to Topher). "Give me five dollars, man."

"Give you five dollars? That's what you want?" It sounded more like a statement than a question. Pasty pulled the hefty revolver from his jacket pocket and pointed it in Anton's face.

"Wait, I—"

Pasty fired his weapon.

§

When Pasty pressed the barrel into Topher's cheek and pulled the trigger, Topher had been expecting to hear the roaring *boom* the weapon made when Pasty shot Anton three times. Instead, the firearm had sounded a metallic *click*. After hearing the tinny sound, Topher bolted for the door.

He wrenched the door open and braced against the rushing wind between the cars. He opened the door of the next car and stumbled through, slipping on the blood dripping from his shoes. The two train coasted to a stop, and the passenger doors opened. Topher flailed and clawed his way through the crowd. He raced up the station steps (taking them two at a time) and burst into the street's light.

Topher ran down the sidewalk, sidestepping oblivious pedestrians. He turned at the end of the block and found himself at the security door of his mother's building. He couldn't seem to find the right apartment number, and he mashed all the buttons at once, buzzing every occupant's room over and over. The security door opened, and he, still in a daze, stumbled up the stairs. When he reached his mother's apartment, he found her standing in the doorway, waiting.

She was wearing her old pink robe, and her hair was covered by a blue wrap. The ice clinked in her rocks glass. Topher had never been so happy to smell Jack Daniels and cheap perfume. He reached for his mother, but before he could wrap his arms around her, he felt a piercing, searing pain below his right eye. He saw only white. Then, only black.

Topher was dead, and blood pooled around his body from the gunshot. The two train coasted to a stop, and the passenger doors opened.

MOISÉS R. DELGADO
Excision

I HOLD A HEATED SCALPEL to the edge of my tongue. The basement is crowded and silent, a ring of family and friends stare at the center where I am kneeling, my elbows aimed stiffly at the floor. The crowd—my uncles Nido and Umber, my cousin Brio, the neighbor and his son, Juven and Lento, and other men—watches me and waits to see red dribble down onto my chin, to smell flesh burning, to hear the hiss of a wound being cauterized. Ice cubes in my father's hands crunch as he leans in closer to me. The breath he was withholding is warm in my ear as if meaning to say, *"You can do it . . . Don't disappoint me."* My hand stutters and I nick my tongue without meaning to. I subdue the flinch that would have driven the scalpel into my throat. I feel panic escape my body in the form of horripilation of my skin.

I taste blood.

"Blood and blood," my father signed last night before bed. "Blood is all you can taste for months." Metal, rust, ice burning in mouth. I will eat and I will remember, so I will taste iron, steel, ashes without fire. "But eventually you'll realize that the palate can also taste, that sense of smell is important, and you'll again be able to savor more than just blood."

"I'm nervous," I told him.

"It's normal."

"What if I can't?"

"You will." He gave me a kiss on the cheek. "Tomorrow, Martes, you'll be a man."

"Wait," I said. I didn't want to sleep. "What does it feel like?" I pointed at my mouth, licked the back of my teeth to reassure myself that I hadn't yet done it.

He laughed silently, his mouth an empty cave.

One can still produce sound afterward. My older cousin, Garter, proved it with, "I still can," that came out like Styrofoam rubbing on Styrofoam. But it's like the mind forgets with age. Laughter becomes a few clicks, like a broken radio regaining its signal in short bursts. Clicks then become nothing other than a silent exhale. Maybe disillusion is involved. One can only listen to a broken voice for so long. When I was born, my father had already lost his voice. But his facial expressions remain—they most often do after tongue removal. My father's bared teeth, the dimples at the peaks of his smile, the folds around his eyes . . . It feels wrong. Knowing that my father was once capable of sound—even if incoherent—always makes me feel like I am waiting. Waiting for a dam to burst, for glass to shatter, for a wall to fall and reveal sound.

"At first, you'll feel empty, you'll want to shout," he said. "Scream!" The sign for the word "scream" exaggerated. Like holding an apple in hand near the mouth and extending the arm out. Like grasping onto the worm and forcibly pulling it out of the throat.

Then I had a dream that I was falling with my mouth open. And I awoke this morning feeling like I had a gust of air stuck between my cheeks.

The room stomps their feet in cheer—the children shriek, howl, whoop—for the first cut of the night. For the *fisssh* and bit of steam that leave my mouth. For the smell of cooked meat rising toward the ceiling. They clap for more; their eyes crave for blood to glisten white as it reflects the celadon hue of the light above me.

But I can't continue carving flesh. I ask myself why. *Why can't I?* The pain was bearable—almost pleasing. Euphoric? At the same time, it was the worst thing I've ever felt, like chewing on live embers. Like having someone reach into my mind and tear out all thought.

My father looks at me, a blur of a smile on his face. He gently massages my back with one hand, ice still in the other, assuring me that he, and everyone present, is here in case of anything. He and everyone are watching . . . waiting. *"Don't keep us waiting,"* I imagine him signing. *"You're fourteen today. Be a man!"*

I remember the first time my father put out a cigar on my tongue. I rushed into the bathroom to stare at the mark. A purple-black circle on pink. I convinced myself it was an eye so that I would stop crying. I was seven; it was a Sunday. In two weeks, he'd run the edge of paper on the tip of my tongue until he saw scarlet on my teeth. Every fourteen days he would change from cigar to paper. Though, sometimes there were other things. A hot coal when I turned eight, which I had to lick until my lips were dry and peeling. At age ten there was a rusted nail in my mouth so that I'd familiarize myself with the flavor. And at thirteen I had to use my own teeth, I had to press into my tongue until I made myself bleed.

"Bite your tongue," my father kept signing. "Bite, bite, bite." Fingers repeatedly closing around his index finger and knuckle. His fingernails began to dig into his flesh—he drew blood before I did.

"I'm proud of you," my father signs, poorly, trying to keep ahold of the ice. I can see the worry in the bead of sweat running down the border of his nose. The cubes are melting in the warmth of his brown hands. Soon they will be a puddle of water, and then what if I haven't done it? Will he bring out more ice? Will he smile, say it's normal to be nervous? Will he apologize? Will he stare at the floor? *Why did it have to be my son?* he might think.

If the ice melted again, would he hesitate to cut my throat? Would I be the first in generations of our ancestry to die at fourteen with tongue still in mouth?

"Perhaps it arose from paranoia," my father once told me. *Or maybe from corruption, or from intellect, or from a spiritual message, or from a trip on acid.* But the generally accepted idea is that tongue cutting was initially an act of rebellion.

They say, though evidence is sparse, that a new procedure arose. *Tongue-printing,* my father called it, was intended to prove criminals guilty by transcribing everything a person ever said. Every hello and goodbye, every proclamation of love, every secret whispered into a pillow. But tongue-prints were abused, it is said, so a man hacked at his tongue. Then another man amputated his own tongue, then a gang, then a whole city, and a state. But there is no concrete proof of tongue-printing ever having existed. The act of tongue removal, however, is banned because whether real or not, there are many who believe tongue-printing was real and continue the practice of tongue extraction. If one is caught during the act, one can be sentenced to death for "active participation in a cult." Courts will often deem tongue excision a cruel punishment, one that is often sloppily executed, therefore, ending in many deaths. If found after the procedure, the law will do nothing about it because of how many are without tongue.

"If you're ever asked," my father once signed, "say it was done against your will. They can't prove you're lying."

Maybe it was rebellion, I tell myself... though, without any physical proof in existence, I struggle to fight off all doubt. Maybe it was an accident that for some reason became popular. Maybe a father was bored and wanted to see what a tongue out of body looked like. He wanted to know if it would speak on its own, if he'd develop the symptoms of phantom limb. Then his sons were bored and did the same, then the sons of the sons, and the sons of the sons of the sons . . .

"Doesn't matter. What matters," my father said, "is that it's a part of our culture."

"But . . ."

"Are you ashamed of who we are?"

Was I? *Am I?* I never brought up the topic again.

The room rustles, sighs are exchanged, family and friends shift where they are. The ones standing in the outer circle want to sit, the ones sitting near me want to stand. Like water rippling, a second stone breaking the ring.

My father leans in closer to me, the barely frozen puddle in his hands dampens the ceremonial red robe I wear. He looks at me, my tongue outside my mouth, the scalpel near flesh. He smiles, though I know the last thing he's feeling is joy. It's in the brown of his eyes, the words *"Are you ashamed?"* in bold, thickening the longer he maintains the smile. Letters distilling into one another, losing meaning, losing sound. Just a deafening silence that begs for blood, for disembodied tongue.

I can't, I want to scream. My tongue twitches, the gash from earlier is deepened. A sizzle escapes my mouth, a droplet of crimson inches down my chin.

My father sighs, the crowd around me leans in closer. *"More,"* their breaths seem to say.

I can't, I can't, I can't.

My hand moves without my thought. I taste cigar ashes, rusted nails, dirty paper. My father straightens his back, pushes his chest outward, moves closer to me so everyone remembers that I am his son.

I slash.

Palms meet thighs, emitting a soft *thump, thump, thump,* like thunder in the distance.

Sanguine, sangre, cruor.

Children, those with tongues still intact, laugh, jump in place, roar, hurrah in excitement. They scream the way I want to scream, until my ears squeal because of the intense noise. I want to shout, I want to yell, I want to cry out into the suffocating room—the men around me lean in closer as I cut, creating a wave of red with their robes. A claustrophobic sphere I am trapped in, a darkness that closes in on me.

I can't scream. I can't stop. I cut, I cut, I cut.

I taste blood, see my tongue drop to the floor. The men, the teens, the young boys around me all stand and press into me. And there on the floor beside me, before all light is muted by robed bodies, I see it. A heart without a beat, a swollen rose petal, an unblinking pink eye, a red bird without wings.

MOISÉS R. DELGADO
Perennial

"WHEN YOUR FATHER PASSED AWAY…" my mother said, staring out the balcony at the metallic horizon in the distance. Solar panels on every roof in the city capturing sunrays and mirroring the stonewashed sky above. "I woke up many mornings reaching for him."

Outside, a car zoomed upward toward the apartment's rooftop. A fistful of dirt from my mother's attempt at a garden was swept into the living room. We watched the soil clumsily rise and fall then settle between cracks in the black-tiled floor. And it would probably stay, brown was already wedged between several tiles. My mother often left the balcony doors open and was getting too old to clean everything thoroughly. Yet she wouldn't—

"Somedays I still do," she continued, a shivering hand over her lips. *"Hay días que aun lo extraño."*

"I miss him, too," I said. "But I know he's somewhere—"

"Don't start, Juvenal," my mother said, flustered. She pushed herself out of her seat, legs wobbling until she rested her weight on her walking cane.

The metal rod shifted under her, adjusting and rearranging itself to keep her upright.

I watched her as she stood by the balcony doors. The occasional car flew past, downward, upward, sideways. When close enough, they would send in a gust of grimy wind and flecks of dirt through the slight opening. And my mother would hold onto her silk robe, allow the gust to shake her cold, to disturb the loose gray hairs resting over her wrinkled forehead. After some minutes, she opened the doors completely, removed the filters in her nose, and took in a breath.

I rushed to her side, took the filters from her hand and hurriedly put them back inside her nose.

"Mom," I said, out of breath from jumping out of my seat, "the air is toxic for you!" In the distance, factories huffed out gray clouds, further discoloring the blue sky.

She smiled, laughed shortly, like a spoon gently tapping on a wine glass. "A few seconds won't kill you. I remember when I was three, we—"

"I don't care, Mom," I said. "Times have changed since."

We exchanged silence, looking each other in the eye. Her once brown-black eyes like the bark of a young tree, now washed out like the same bark after years of dry heat, of storms, of critters crawling up and down.

Finally, she said: "I'm old. *Pronto moriré.*"

I hated it. I hated every time she mentioned her death. Like it was nothing. Like it was something we should look forward to with open arms and a smile on our face.

"You don't have to die," I said. "I want you to live. Ma, *por favor—*"

"Stop," she said, a hand at her throat. She was breathing heavily. "I don't want to . . . I've told you. I've told you not to bring it up."

"*Por favor,* Ma. You can be young again. And, your body will be able to breathe without the filters. If only you—"

"I can do that now." Her breathing was back to normal.

"But if you breathe it in, the air slowly kills you. But if—"

"Age will kill me first."

"We could be together forever. Just agree to—"

"I don't want to be forever!" she said.

She was shivering, breathing hard, shaking her head. I managed to catch her as her cane slipped from her hand and her legs gave away. I helped her to the sofa. Watched as the fear trembled out of her body. As she struggled to regain her normal breathing.

"I'm sorry," I said. "I just—"

"Enough," she said. "I understand how you feel. But . . . do you know why I keep tending to my garden even though everything fails to grow?"

I shook my head.

"Because it reminds me that all ends."

"Are you not afraid?"

"I'm afraid," she said, a hand over her chest, "that the day will arrive, and I'll still be breathing."

"I love you, Ma."

"I love you, too," she said, her eyes trained on the stalk of a growing flower. I followed her gaze, saw the green blade shiver and be dragged away by the wind.

JIM FIELDS
Hot and Crispy

"TWO FRIES LEFT!" THE HISPANIC guy shouted. His voice had an urgency that belonged to only the most dedicated of fast food workers. Jermaine couldn't remember the kid's name, not that it mattered. It was 11:30 in the morning and Jermaine stood at his post at Burger Bites. At twenty-eight, Jermaine worked as the fryer specialist at their flagship location in Midtown Omaha. He stared down into the baskets of frozen fries as they cooked in a vat of boiling grease. The noon lunch rush was in full swing, and Jermaine was behind as usual because he couldn't stop his persistent thoughts. *I hate this place. Why am I still here?* He stood over the stainless-steel vat of boiling grease and made French fries and onion rings all day while his pimply faced teenage colleagues bagged orders and scurried about the kitchen. Even though it was less than a year old, Burger Bites was the most popular lunch spot in town.

Burger Bites were small bite-sized hamburgers that were the size of a pizza roll. Served on a special mini-bun, the burgers came with a wide variety of toppings like Italian, Mexican, Chinese, and scrambled egg, which was popular at breakfast. There was even a dessert bite that mixed ground beef with chocolate and whipped cream. Customers never bought just one; the company sold them by the pound, allowing people to mix and match all sorts of different flavors. At first, there was just one location in West Omaha, Nebraska, but the mini-burgers caught on and before long Burger Bites sprouted up all over the city and then throughout the Midwest. Now, the company was on the verge of becoming a national chain. *Why do I know this useless information?* Then Jermaine remembered it had been required in order to get hired. That was six months ago. *If only I didn't need the money. I'd disappear like spit on a griddle.*

But at night, everything was different. Jermaine played jazz guitar as part of a band at The Blue Flamingo club in North Omaha. But jazz didn't pay. Not in Nebraska. If you were lucky enough to make a living as a musician in the Midwest, you either played classic dad rock in a slick cover band or you played schmaltzy old standards and polkas in a wedding show band. Neither one appealed to Jermaine. He was too much of a purist. The night before, at The Blue Flamingo, Jermaine played his heart out for five hours and only made thirteen dollars. But that wasn't the point. Jermaine knew he needed to continue to refine his craft, so he practiced hard for three or more hours every morning before work, learning from the masters by playing their records over and over, playing along with the worn-out old jazz albums his father had left before he took off for good. And then, Jermaine had the cassette tapes Billy sent him from New York.

Billy was a local tenor sax player who had made it. Frustrated by the limited opportunities for jazz musicians in the Midwest, Billy had hitchhiked his way to New York City when he was just a teenager. Now, twenty years later, Billy made thousands of dollars a week as a session musician. He was on all of the new albums from the best jazz artists. Billy had made it, and someday Jermaine, too, would pack up and head for New York. *But not yet. I'm not ready.*

"You're out of fries!" cried the Hispanic cook in a panic. Muttering something in Spanish, he gave Jermaine a look of sheer panic as the unfilled orders blinked on the monitor over him. Coming back to reality, Jermaine realized the two baskets of fries he was cooking were done, but the onion rings needed more time.

Expertly, Jermaine lifted each basket out of the fryer, shook the grease out of each one and then dumped the contents of each basket into a large silver metal tray where they sat under a heat lamp. Next, Jermaine salted the entire tray of fries and began bagging them by using a scoop that always felt awkward in his hand. The kitchen was very hot, and Jermaine's shirt was soaked through with both sweat and splatters of grease from the fryer. Unfortunately, the owner refused to let the staff turn the air conditioner in the back kitchen below seventy degrees, so with the fryers, ovens, and grills on, it was always hot. *A living hell.* Besides the Hispanic cook, there were three black girls who took orders, helped prep the food, and kept the dining area clean. Two of them already had kids, even though they were only sixteen. And they took it all so seriously! Everyone there did, especially the manager, Andrea, the only white person on the staff and a real bitch. And here she came, walking over to his station with a look of determination and disgust.

"Jermaine!" she said. "You've let the onion rings burn again! Pay attention! Every time you burn something you cost the company money!" She held a burnt ring up to his face to make her point.

But Jermaine could care less about costing the company money. He knew that Andrea knew that too. She gave Jermaine a look of disgust and said, "These other fries are done, dump them."

Dutifully, Jermaine did, and as he began bagging the latest batch of fries, Andrea began eating them. Jermaine was convinced that her massive gut and fat ass were proof that *she* was the one costing the company money. Everybody was constantly telling Jermaine how his mistakes were costing the company money, and yet, everybody was always eating the company's food without paying for it. Andrea munched on more fries than Jermaine could bag in an hour, and Latisha, the cashier, a short and plump cube with legs, ate more burger bites than she served. The Hispanic cook, whose name Jermaine could never remember, was grotesquely overweight and had tree trunks for thighs but also had small feminine hands. Andrea ate another handful of fries; then Latisha came over and ate a few more, which made sense since she was pregnant again.

"You better put another basket down," Andrea said as she walked away from Jermaine's station. "And watch them this time!" Jermaine wiped his brow and looked over at the clock. It was only twelve thirty.

As he worked, Jermaine's mind began drifting to the music from last night. He was short, only five foot six, and his guitar was as big as his chest, and yet, there was never any doubt that Jermaine was in control. His fingers moved quickly and efficiently, his right hand moving up and down the fret board like an elevator on speed. When Jermaine was younger, he had the enthusiasm, but not the skill.

Back then, Jermaine was determined to make his living as a professional musician. It wasn't easy. The local hip-hop and rap bands didn't need a guitarist; they relied on DJs and drum machines to make their music groove. In contrast, the classic rock cover bands didn't like the way Jermaine improvised; they wanted everything to sound "just like the record." He ended up working in mostly schmaltzy show bands that were popular at wedding receptions and in the lounges of the city's old Italian steakhouses. Forced to curtail his creativity, Jermaine suffered through them night after night. It was hard. These bands played mostly Elvis and Johnny Cash tunes, along with standards like "The Way We Were." The last band Jermaine played in was run by an accordion player who could only play with one hand. And if a song had more than three chords, the accordion player would cut out most of the chords. Playing "As Time Goes By" with only three chords was not something Jermaine liked to do, no matter how much the gig paid.

Playing songs wrong night after night ruined Jermaine's love of music, so he gave it up. Jermaine decided he would get a regular job. However, with only a high school education and no transportation in a city that relied on cars, Jermaine found his job options were few. At least Burger Bites was on the bus route. Broke, Jermaine moved back home. "It's only temporary," he told his mother. *That was two years ago.*

Home was in the heart of North Omaha—commonly known as the ghetto. The only furniture in the house was a couch with three broken legs propped up by books. The walls were bare except for the streaks from the rain that ran down from the ceiling. His mother had sold his old bed long ago, so Jermaine slept on an air mattress. His only belongings were his guitar, amp, a cassette player, and the old stereo and jazz albums his father had left behind when he took off with another woman back when Jermaine was three.

After work each night, Jermaine sat in his room for hours, practicing, while his aging mother sat in the living room watching televangelists on their ten-inch TV that sat on a milk crate. After a few months of hard work, Jermaine transcended the technical aspects of guitar playing and began expressing his soul through music. His yearning, feelings, and ideas were reflected in the sounds that came from his fingers on the strings, and he soon regained his love of playing music. When Jermaine learned that The Blue Flamingo had hired a jazz band to play there nightly and had a weekly jam session, he decided to check it out. That's when Jermaine blew everybody away. Nobody had heard of him before that night; now, nobody could forget the amazing kid whose guitar was as big as he was and could play like Wes Montgomery himself.

After his blazing performance, Jermaine met Billy, who was visiting from out of town. Billy had grown up only a few blocks from where Jermaine's mother lived. He was a tall, muscular, saxophone player who looked half his age and always dressed sharp. Although he had to leave the next day to return to Manhattan, Billy became Jermaine's mentor, sending him tapes and music charts almost every week. The last time Billy came back to visit, he watched Jermaine tear through a brilliant rendition of the classic standard, "Body and Soul," improvising his way around the melody like a prizefighter in the ring. Billy was impressed and urged Jermaine to come back to New York with him.

"Why the hell do you stay here?" Billy said as they drank whiskeys at the bar. "I mean, you is so *bad* you could kick ass in any city, especially the Big Apple."

Jermaine shook his head. "I'm just not ready."

"Bullshit," Billy said. "What's keeping you here? Your career in fast food?"

Jermaine grimaced. *What was keeping him here?*

Now, as Jermaine stared into the vat of French fries cooking in grease, he realized one day he was going to have to do something and maybe soon. This routine of hot jazz by night and hot fries by day couldn't continue much longer. Suddenly, Andrea ran into the kitchen.

"Stand tall, everyone. Rod's here!"

Rod was the owner of all the Burger Bites. Approaching forty, he was one of those good-looking swimmer types with blond hair. Through the window, Jermaine watched Rod get out of his ketchup-red Porsche. The license plate read "BITE ME."

"You've only got two fries left!" Latisha shouted. "We need more now."

Jermaine grabbed the two baskets of fries that were cooking, dumped them into the tray, salted them, and hurriedly began bagging them with the scoop. He paid careful attention to get just the right amount of fries in each bag; when he first started, Jermaine was always getting into trouble for filling the bags completely full. "Portion control equals profits," Andrea used to tell him. Then she would eat a bag's worth of fries from the warming tray.

"You're out of onion rings!" someone shouted from the front counter.

Oh Christ. Jermaine hated onion rings. They had to be bagged by hand and the rings were always so hot they always burned his fingers, which always hurt later at night when he played guitar at the club. Even so, Jermaine filled a basket with uncooked rings from the bag in the freezer and lowered the basket into the fryer as Rod entered the kitchen and walked over to Jermaine's station. Rod was holding an order of French fries that had already been served.

"Jermaine, look at these fries," Rod said as he shoved the bag of French fries under Jermaine's nose. "Is this how we serve fries here at Burger Bites?"

"They look all right to me."

"They do, huh?" Rod said, his face turning red in anger. "Well, *feel* them." Rod grabbed Jermaine's arm and dumped the fries into his hand.

"They're cold."

"Yes, they are," Rod said. "And why is that?"

Jermaine didn't know what to say, so he stood silent.

"Look, Jermaine. I'm just going to say two words to you—hot and crispy. That's what I want. *Hot and crispy.* Got it?"

Jermaine nodded his head yes, hoping this would appease Rod and he'd go away and leave him alone. But it wasn't going to be that easy.

"Ok, good," Rod said. "Now, I want you to say it. How do I want my fries?"

Jermaine wasn't sure if Rod was treating him like a moron or not, but he made a big grin and with fake enthusiasm said, "Hot and crispy. That's how we serve our fries here at Burger Bites. Hot and Crispy." Rod was not amused.

"Are you mocking me, boy?"

Jermaine shook his head no, even though he was mad as hell. Did Rod really just call him "boy"? *Keep it up and I'll sue your cracker ass.* Meanwhile, Andrea entered the kitchen.

"Do you smell that? Something's burning."

Jermaine had forgotten about the onion rings. Before he could do anything, Rod pushed him aside, took out the basket of burnt black rings and threw them into the trash where they looked like a pile of charcoal. The other baskets had also been frying too long, and Jermaine could see the fries were not "golden brown" as described on the menu but burnt black too.

"What does this mean, boy?" Rod asked as he stared at Jermaine. "Either you're a totally incompetent twenty-eight-year-old moron, or you did this to make me look like a fool."

Everyone in the kitchen was staring at Jermaine. Even in the dining room, the customers waiting in line were staring at him through the front counter window. Without thinking, Jermaine looked Rod in the eye and said, "You can stick your hot and crispy fries up your ass until you shit out onion rings!"

As Jermaine stormed out of the kitchen, he tossed his official Burger Bites baseball cap into the air and it landed on the grill where it started to sizzle. Next, Jermaine took off his apron and tossed it at Andrea, but it landed in the fryer, disappearing under the boiling grease. Then, to make things complete, Jermaine took off his stained, sweaty green Burger Bites polo shirt uniform and tossed it in Rod's face. Jermaine hoped the owner got a good whiff of Jermaine's body odor and sweat.

Rod followed Jermaine out of the back door of the kitchen and into the parking lot. "You come back here! I'm not through yet! This is lost profits! This is deliberate destruction of company property! There are forms to fill out!"

Later, as Jermaine waited for his bus to go home, he wondered where his life was going. *Nowhere.* Jermaine's only hope was to leave the Midwest and go stay with Billy in New York.

Jermaine got off the bus on Twenty-Fourth and Lake and walked the rest of the way home. Billy said that back in the day there were jazz clubs all up and down the street and that Count Basie and Louis Armstrong played there often. Now, all that remained was The Blue Flamingo. All of the other buildings were boarded up or half demolished. It was a shame. Once inside the house, Jermaine grabbed a beer from the fridge and went into his room. He put on his favorite Lester Young album and listened to it as he slowly drank from the bottle. Eventually, the phone rang. Jermaine answered it, dreading it was someone from Burger Bites.

"Hello?"

"He's dead," a female voice said.

"What? Who's dead?" Jermaine thought the caller must have a wrong number or something.

"Billy. Billy Rodgers. They found him in his apartment in Brooklyn. He was supposed to be at a recording session downtown. The record producer got worried, so they went over there." The female voice began sobbing.

"Oh my God." Jermaine's head spun with the news. Then it occurred to him that he didn't recognize the female voice on the other end of the line. "Who are you?"

"I'm his sister, Lavonne."

"So what happened? Did he have a heart attack?" Jermaine suddenly felt dizzy.

"No. They think it was an overdose. Heroin. The funeral is Wednesday. Of course, you won't be able to make it, but I wanted you to know."

"Thanks," Jermaine mumbled. He could hear Lavonne crying on the other end of the line. He wondered if she could hear him crying too.

"I've got to go now," she finally said. "I've got to call other people."

"OK," Jermaine replied, hanging up the phone. Jermaine's head whirled as he collapsed on the old air mattress that served as his bed. He let out a deep breath. Eventually, hopelessness gave way to resolve. It was time to move on, and no matter what happened, Jermaine would find a way. Not just for Billy, but for himself too.

KARA GALL
The Body That Dares

BRENDA SHAKES AN ELLIPTICAL PILL from an orange-tinted plastic bottle. She reaches her arm straight out in front of her face and squeezes the light beige soft gel between her thumb and middle finger. "I'm crushing your head," she says in a vaguely eastern European accent to her reflection in the mirror.

She laughs once—to herself. There isn't anyone home to remember the meme that came before the Internet, tucked away in her brain for decades. She takes a deep breath in, closes her eyes, and retracts her hand until she can feel the heat of it an inch from the bridge of her nose. She makes a bet with herself. The mail-order pharmacy sends three months of progesterone at a time, and each bottle often contains pills from multiple manufacturers. She likes to test her intuition by guessing the pill imprint code. "AK2," she whispers. She opens her eyes and frowns. P2. She fills the bathroom cup, chases the medicine with tap water.

A minute later, her phone buzzes. A text from her husband. "Did you take your pill?"

"Took it," she writes back. He had been the one to set up the reminder on her phone, showed her how to choose the sound, how to set start and end dates. From now until eternity, days one through twelve of each month were dedicated to the scientific principle that unopposed estrogen is a bad thing, a fact ceremoniously rung into her consciousness at 8:30 p.m. with a Tibetan bowl chime.

"Did you eat?" he asks next.

Months ago—on a night like tonight, when he worked late and she made dinner and kept it warm for him—she took the pill right at 8:30, as soon as her phone alarm chimed, expecting him to arrive home shortly. But there had been traffic, or an accident, or a last-minute request from the boss, or something she didn't try to imagine, that delayed his arrival. She put a plate over the rice to keep it warm, left the lowest flame burning under the cube steak. She sat at the dining table waiting for him, pushing her place setting aside and blinking through emails on her phone as a drowsy buzzed feeling of well-being spread up from her chest and doubled her vision. When she heard his key in the front door at 9:15, she stood from the table and walked to the stove. She picked up the pot of rice, her head beginning to spin. At the threshold between kitchen and dining room, her toes caught on the transition molding between tile and wood. She instinctively reached out, the pan swinging from her arms like a bowling ball, rolling through the dining room on a trajectory toward the back hallway, rice grains rippling across the grain of oak-like river sediment. She was too late to catch herself.

Rather than crying out in pain or cursing—both responses that would not have surprised her husband—she convulsed with laughter. "I'm the sower! I'm casting the seeds of my life to the wind!"

"What the hell, Brenda?" he said, dropping his briefcase and running to the dining room, crouching next to her. "Are you OK? Have you been drinking?"

"Nope," she slurred as he tried to help her up from the ground. "I'm *progesta*-drunk."

He had attributed the buzz to an empty stomach, read about it on a forum online, and now made sure to always ask her if she had eaten. She wonders if he programmed alarms into his own phone.

That night's side effects had not been a total surprise to her—though she hadn't anticipated the exacerbated, quickened effects. For a few months now, she had noticed a pattern. About an hour after taking the pill, her vision would start to blur, her eyes grow heavy. A deep contentedness would fill her chest, and she felt too large for their small living room with its floral-patterned wallpaper and cornered television.

"I think I'll head to bed," she would say to him from her recliner, handing him the remote, offering him a quick kiss. If she didn't time it correctly, when she went to brush her teeth, she would stumble into the walls like a pinball machine, giggling the whole way, relying on his increasingly diminished hearing to keep her secret. For about twenty minutes each night, she lay in bed, the progesterone high lapping at her senses, each sound and sensation existing for her amusement. She felt present for the high of it, blissfully detached from side effects, unexplained bruises and ruined dinners aside. It was a little like being drunk, without the pounding heart and irritation, without the sense of being ejected from her own body. She could not remember the last time she was inebriated, which was probably for the best. The night she met her husband, so many decades ago? The night they conceived their daughter, their only child, gone two years now to a college town nestled between mountain and ocean, thousands of miles from home? Naturally, Brenda stopped drinking when she found out she was pregnant, and since then she can remember having no more than a glass of wine at social events.

Even now, as her husband asks if she has eaten, she can feel the edge of the buzz. It will be a fast transition, like her daughter's birth, not much warning, especially on an empty stomach. She taps out a response on her phone. "Not yet. Waiting for you."

"Go ahead and eat," he writes. "I'm going to be late. Hoping to be home around ten."

"OK," she writes. "Tired. Will go to bed after I eat. Plate in oven for you."

She makes him a plate, mashed potatoes with a few slices of roast, some roasted carrots and onions on the side. She puts it in the oven and takes out another plate, smears a teaspoon of mashed potato on it with a few fibers of roast and a stray onion. She rubs them all together on the plate, and then leaves it, unwashed, in the sink.

She makes herself a cup of nettle tea, harvested herself from a country road ditch. She clamps the stainless-steel snap-ball tea infuser around the dried leaves, pours boiling water over the top, and steeps it in a mug from a place she's never been. She likes the ceramic heft of it, the way her palm fits between handle and cup.

In their bedroom, she peels off her sweatpants, examines herself in the mirror. She tests her profile, hikes up the pouchy overhang of skin that drapes from her stomach, holds it up with one forearm, while lifting her breasts with the other. *I'm not obese*, she thinks, despite what the BMI report said, printed on her last doctor's visit summary in the same all-caps black text the pharmaceutical companies used. She just had too much extra skin that had somehow come unanchored from the fascia beneath.

She sips the tea, then lets the rounded end of the infuser rest between her lips, touches the tip of it with her tongue. She opens her mouth slightly, rotates her head in circles so that the metal grazes the borders of her lips. She laughs at herself, places the mug carefully on the nightstand and flops naked on the bed, laughing some more. She turns on the bedroom television, flips through the channels, closing one eye to circumvent her double vision, so that she can watch the shows, the ones where the women's breasts ride high like Olivia Hussey's in Franco Zeffirelli's *Romeo and Juliet*. And the others, too, the ones in Brooklyn, an urban landscape foreign to her, real lives of people in places she will never know.

When she can't keep her eyes open anymore, she turns off the television, takes another sip of tea, tugs the flannel sheet to her ears. She shimmies one of the extra pillows under the covers, into the space between her side of the bed and her husband's. She wraps her arms around it and pulls it close. In her head, she says a prayer for the daughter gone off to college, the beautiful woman of a daughter who stands on the shoulders of two generations of sexual liberation, the daughter whose woman body is more beautiful than she possibly knows, at least in this decade. The body that hikes ridges and scavenges sands, the body that ebbs and flows in hormonal tides, the body that dares. Even in her sleep, Brenda smiles. In the morning, she will wake up without a hangover, feeling fully rested, fully feeling the weight of her breasts and belly. Wishing for someone to hold them up.

JaLEAH HEDRICK
Bulldog and Blues

IT'S COLD OUT WHEN I GET to her house. I fumble through her key ring, trying each in the lock. I can hear the bulldog scrambling against the inside of the door—he must think I'm her.

Yesterday, I was eating at an Applebee's when a phone call flooded my world with grief. My best friend Afina had collapsed at work. I didn't need to hear any more. I knew by the sound of her dad's voice that I was never going to see her again. But I listened. It was a blood clot. A little bit of coagulated blood that had slipped into her lung and taken her away from me.

"I couldn't get a flight out until Friday," he told me, "But the dog . . ."

The lights are already on inside. This little old house has always had a dusty quality, and her mishmash of thrift finds only amplifies it. Afina came to this city for art school, and I came with her for the change of scenery. She moved into this house after I moved in with my boyfriend. Unbidden, laments of how little I'd seen the place in the last year fill my head.

I tell the frantically circling dog to calm down, but he doesn't. We follow each other to the kitchen, me carrying my canvas grocery bag. He leads me right to his food bowl, which I drop into the bag. I dump his water and stow that bowl as well. Above the sink, in a doorless cabinet, sits an abstract display of dog food and treats: cans, pouches, a big paper bag. I sweep the lot of it into the tote, but a few cans clatter to the floor, exploding the kitchen with noise. The dog grunts and trots away.

As I'm picking them up, something catches my eye. Drip marks. Ocean-colored paint in sharp relief on the worn hardwood. They must have rained from her. She must have been painting! I follow smears of that same blue-gray up the banister, with the dog on my heels. Her studio door on the landing is closed. The blustery paint on the doorknob hasn't completely set.

It's rubbery. Whatever she was painting, it had to have been recent.

Inside, a ruby armchair faces an easel. I don't know what I hoped to find. Something. Something new. But the easel is empty. I squint around in the natural light from the high windows on the back wall and notice the floor is littered with the curled peels of a blood orange. The dog laps one of them up and lowers his head to slop at it. I kneel down too. He probably shouldn't eat them. Gathering them up, I see they are marked with the same paint. They are strange in my hand, like thick petals from some exotic plant. Eyes adjusting, I take them to the windowsill, hoping it's out of the dog's reach.

Outside, the bare ribs of the trees are sketched across the bleached late-autumn sky. A soft blue set of fingerprints has been pressed onto the windowpane over this backdrop. All five, spread in their imperfect semicircle.

JEN IPPENSEN
Small-Town Still

WE SLIPPED OUT THE SIDE DOOR and walked the two blocks to the park, passing under one weak streetlamp, hearing bugs zap over the bulb's constant hum, accidentally bumping shoulders now and then but not really touching. I glanced back once, but no one followed. The night was small-town still.

At the swing set, Carl stopped and cupped his hand. A flame flickered over his face, and he looked both beautiful and terrifying. We passed the joint back and forth, taking turns holding our breath and blowing smoke into the near silence.

He pulled tall, brown grass strands that sprouted up around the swing set supports, tossing them in the air over my head, while I swatted at them like mad. We laughed, and our sounds floated up, forming a bubble around us. No one could find us if they came looking; we had a secret sound barrier. I hopped on a swing and pumped my legs to get started. When Carl did an underdoggy, I screeched, breaking the barrier, and the sound bounced back at us from every surface—merry-go-round, monkey bars, picnic tables, tornado slide.

"Shh." He cast a glance down the street. His eyes were wide and smiling, but he said, "We don't want anyone coming for us."

He bummed a Marlboro Light. We couldn't sync up, so our cherries crisscrossed as we swung. I tired of kicking and slowed to a stop, planting my feet in the dirt. Carl pumped hard and jumped off at the highest point. He landed with a thud.

His cherry burned in the grass behind him as he walked toward me, and I wondered if the dry grass would burn, and if it did, would he put it out?

He grabbed my legs and wrapped them around his hips, still a perfect fit. I put my hand on his chest and felt his shirt damp with cold sweat, rising and falling. I thought I could feel his heart pounding, but it could have been my own pulse throbbing in my fingertips.

That tiny ember caught my eye and somehow brought to mind when I overheard his father saying I'm the kind of girl you screw around with but not the kind you marry, and the long silence when Carl didn't say otherwise. I waited for him in their foyer, feeling small under the vaulted ceiling.

"I like coming here alone sometimes," he said.

"I can head back if you want," I offered.

He held my thighs tighter, squeezing our sound barrier back into existence. I crossed my ankles behind him, pulled him closer, pulled the barrier down around us, and the night compressed. He pressed his forehead against mine, and I felt his breath, warm on my lips. I thought of how many times we'd been through this and sighed. When I leaned back and uncrossed my ankles, he ran his hands along the length of my legs, leaving a chill behind.

"Well, I guess we should go," he said.

Picking at a cuticle, I thought of my dad's nails outlined in grease and how he must wipe his hands on his coveralls before taking the keys from Carl's dad when he drops off his Cadillac Escalade for an oil change.

"You go on ahead," I told him.

I watched until he passed under the streetlamp, then I crossed to the slide. I held tight to the cool aluminum frame as I climbed to the top. I sat on the platform, listening as the small-town stillness embraced me. Then, with no one there to stop me, I sang out into the night.

NICOLE KONECK-WILWERDING
Overgrown

JERRY KNEW THAT THE PEACH TREE had to come down. Its branches hung low and heavy, bursting with so much fruit that the trunk had started to split down the middle. The sun beat down and the air hummed with songs from cicadas that had forgotten to go back underground and crickets that hid in the shade of the strawberry plants. The roses bloomed by the memorial bench erected in the honor of a past gardener. The sunflowers on the southeast corner hung their heads, heavy with seeds, and Jerry could smell oncoming rain in the wind.

Jerry had started the community garden in the empty corner lot next to his house with the goal of creating such a warm, noisy oasis and to keep teenagers from breaking bottles on the curb and scaring his dogs at night. His daughter, Michelle, had spent most of her afternoons that summer in the lot with him, wiping sweat from her downy blonde brow, reminding him to put sunscreen on. Only eight years old then and a hell of a green thumb, she had been the one who found the dwarf peach tree in a forgotten corner of the local nursery, its small, banana-shaped leaves withering in the hot sun. The peach tree had been the first thing Jerry planted, and the gardeners had made the peaches into pies, jams, and jellies. Still, the trunk seemed to tilt under the weight of its fruit; Jerry had not kept up with trimming the branches each season, and a decision had to be made.

Jerry lit a cigarette and leaned against a fence post to consider his options. He could post to the community garden Facebook group and ask for a group of volunteers to help take the tree down; someone would have to be there to take the peaches home. He couldn't eat them all. His daughter would want to can some, he knew, but she wouldn't be at his place for the rest of the summer. She had decided to stay in California with his ex.

He could take it down himself or ask his brother to help. Rudy usually didn't have anything going on, but Rudy would say, only half-joking, "It's a *community* garden, right? So, ask the community before you ask me."

"Those bastards won't help," Jerry muttered. Only three people had shown up to freshen the mulch between each plot when the farm supply company had accidentally delivered it early and blocked off his driveway for three days. Two families had signed up at the beginning of the spring but never planted anything, even though they had gathered around the picnic tables one cool April morning with the rest of the gardeners to drink bad coffee out of Styrofoam cups and go over their gardening goals for the year. He had to take over their plots and fill them with tomatoes and beans. He had to mow the lawn each Sunday. He had to buy the special solar lights and the signs for each plot. At night, he would drink a beer on his porch and look at the tic-tac-toe patterns the solar lights made, admiring everything he had done that week, cursing everyone who failed to show up and tend the soil.

He ground out his cigarette on one of the old picnic tables and sat. The peaches were huge and lush, and he knew there would be backlash against his decision either way. The tree blocked Plot A5's sun, and the owners of Plot C5 had informed him that the sap that ran from the peach tree would kill anything growing beneath it. "Why'd you even plant it in the first place?" the head gardener for C5 demanded. Jerry couldn't remember the guy's name, just that he had a gray beard and usually wore sunglasses with a bandana. Jerry had still been a little drunk the morning of their meet and greet.

One girl, a jumpy hipster type who wanted to "plant some seeds of peace in her soul," had been pissed that there were Styrofoam cups at the greeting day. Styrofoam "defeated the entire point" of a community garden. She had stood a little apart from the rest of them; with Michelle gone for the year, she was by far the youngest gardener there. She had plot E4. Jerry always looked out his living room window to see if she was out there with her cutting knife and square-shaped glasses before he ventured out to do his work.

Jerry could never tell if she was being ironic or not. He wanted to ask Michelle if "seeds of peace" was a common phrase her generation used these days but shook his head. His daughter already thought he was out of touch.

He wiped his hands on his sweat-drenched khaki shorts and dug his phone out of one of the deep pockets. The phone rang twice. "Rudy," he said. "You got a minute?"

Rudy sighed. Jerry knew that he always had a minute.

§

He decided to call Michelle next, to let her know that her pet plant would be coming down, but he only reached her voicemail again. He leaned against the rain barrel and scrolled through her Instagram while he waited for Rudy to arrive. There she was with her arms around a strange boy who wore a stud in his ear; there she was with her blonde hair shaved on one side of her head; there she was smoking in a dim bookstore. He kept scrolling, two weeks back, then a month, then two months, then three . . . She never seemed to go outside anymore.

§

The problem was that neither of them had taken down a tree before. "Well," said Rudy as he placed his hands on his hips. "Do we pick the fruit first?"

"Maybe," Jerry said. He wiped sweat off his forehead. Rudy had only been outside ten minutes and already his bald head was as red as his T-shirt, his tall white socks dirtied from walking through the grass instead of the garden paths. Jerry tugged down his own tank top, grateful that he was wearing black, so the sweat wouldn't show. "I think I got some pallet boxes in the garage to pack them in."

"You need help getting them?" Rudy asked.

Jerry sighed. "Is that your way of saying we should pick the fruit first?"

Rudy pushed his glasses up his nose. "I guess. Just seems a waste if we don't."

Jerry led the way. He unhooked the garden gate to let Rudy through, relatched it, and then guided Rudy through his own messy backyard. Two of the four dogs were out, the rottweiler-lab mix and the Australian cattle dog that only had half an ear. They barreled toward Rudy who greeted them each warmly, running his hands over their ears and necks, crooning, "Hi, babies. Yes, you're big babies."

"The ex is scared of that one," Jerry said, nodding his head at the rottweiler mix. "She keeps bugging me to get rid of him every time she drops Michelle off. But she hasn't done that in a year."

"Michelle's in California for the summer?" Rudy asked, still petting the dogs as he squinted at his brother. "I thought you got summers."

"I did get summers, but she met a boy," Jerry said, shrugging. "She'll come in for the state fair, though."

"That'll be good," said Rudy.

"Yeah." Jerry watched his older brother. Nearly sixty years old, and all it took was a pair of mutts to get him smiling. Jerry fished around in his pocket for another cigarette but found none. He checked his watch. Three in the afternoon. Too early for whiskey.

"If you want to open the garage up, I'm going to grab a beer," he said. Rudy nodded, still distracted by the dogs. They each tried to knock the other out of the way, so they could lean against Rudy's legs. Jerry snorted. "You want the rest of them out here? Usually I let all four out, but the big guy's been snapping at the beagle."

"No, we don't want any fights," Rudy said. His glasses flashed in the sunlight. "You go on, I'll get the boxes."

Jerry sighed in the cool blankness of his white kitchen. The beagle and the border collie ran to greet him, panting, their eyes bright with expectation. He looked at their water bowl and noticed it was empty, so he refilled it and set it down. He filled a glass of water for himself and drank it. Then he had another. He didn't need a beer, but it was hot, and he was about to do some hard work. Why not make it a little easier?

The dogs lapped at the water, spilling most of it onto the tile floor. "Should probably get some for your brothers out there, eh?" He looked out the kitchen window to see that Rudy had beat him to it. Instead of getting the boxes ready, Rudy had unwound the hose and was offering a stream of (probably lead-laced) water to the dogs.

Jerry opened the fridge and considered his options. A stout would be too heavy, but a Bud Light would be too weak. He found some IPAs towards the back and grabbed two, even though he knew that Rudy would say no.

The bottle opener wasn't in its usual place. Jerry ran a hand through his hair, trying not to notice that his own hairline was receding. He was fifty-three and knew his hair would be gone sometime, but he wasn't ready for it yet.

"Okay, think," he told himself. "Where would you put it?"

He padded around the living room and found three still-sticky cut-glass whiskey tumblers and a wine opener with half a cork still stuck to it. "Dark in here," he muttered, opening the blinds. The two dogs followed him around, still grinning. The beagle hopped up on the couch to look out at the street through the front windows.

He went upstairs, carrying the two sweating bottles by the neck, scanning the floor. Had he had a beer last night before bed? Or had that been Thursday?

There was another whiskey tumbler on his bedside table and a full pack of cigarettes. "Nice," he said, swiping them. He went on into the bathroom and set the beers down on the countertop. The bathroom was above the kitchen and had a window that faced his backyard. He glanced out to see that Rudy had started getting the boxes out for the peaches. "I gotta get a move on," he said out loud. The collie sat in the doorway between bedroom and bathroom and smiled at him. He fumbled with his belt buckle—*better piss now, who knows how long this will take*—and saw the bottle opener laying on top of the dusty toilet tank.

"Bingo," he said. He tried to pee but there was nothing. "Sweating too much today, girlie," he told the collie. She grinned, and he zipped and put the bottle opener in his back pocket. "Cheers," he said, walking past her. "What do you think, is it your turn to be outside?"

§

There were too many peaches, ripe and ready to go. Rudy had stacked the boxes around the perimeter of the tree, and Jerry stood on one of the rickety ladders someone had donated to the garden shed, gathering fruit and passing it to Rudy, who placed each one gently in a box. E4 hipster girl had shown up and stomped straight to her plot without saying hello. She had brought her own clipping shears and a canvas tote bag with a *New Yorker* stamp on it.

"Pass it," Jerry said, and Rudy handed him the open IPA. The other bottle rested in the shade. Jerry took a long drink. "Better finish this one before that second one gets too hot," he said, passing the bottle back to Rudy.

"I can run it in the house if you want," Rudy offered.

"Nah," he said. Out of the corner of his eye, he saw hipster girl frowning at the pair of them. He leaned down, swaying on the ladder a bit, and half-whispered, "Do you think she reads the *New Yorker*, or did she steal that bag from her mom?"

Rudy shrugged. "She probably reads it. I read their free articles online when I can."

"It costs sixty bucks a month to get it delivered here. It's the Midwest, aren't they flying over us all the time anyway?"

"Pick some peaches."

"I hate the East Coast."

"You've never been. Besides," Rudy added, lowering his voice, "she's from Hastings. Had a rough time."

"Jesus Christ, I bet," Jerry said, laughing. "Who would live in Hastings?" He reached back up into the tree for a peach.

"You talking about me?" the girl called.

"No," Jerry shouted back. "Hello to you too, by the way."

"Hi," Rudy said, smiling and waving to the girl. "What's your problem?" he hissed at Jerry.

"Nothing, just this is a *community* garden, only the *community* doesn't give a shit!" Jerry said loudly, waving his arms. "Everyone's critical, no one says hello—"

"Oh my god," the girl said. "You were talking about Hastings, I heard you."

"I barely said anything about Hastings," Jerry sneered.

"Well, I'm from there," the girl insisted, throwing her shears to the ground and pointing at her chest. "I'm just here to plant some things and weed and relax, and you're taking all the peaches for yourself."

Rudy cleared his throat the way he did when he wanted to explain something, but something in Jerry snapped. He hopped off the ladder and stomped towards her, shaking his finger. "I don't even know who you are! You're E5!"

"Fuck you, I'm E4," said the girl. She bent to pick up her shears and her tote bag and stalked off.

Rudy pushed his glasses up the bridge of his nose and glared at Jerry. "What was that all about?"

"Never mind." Jerry picked up the IPA and drained it, then dropped it to the ground so he could crack open the next one. "Let's just get this taken care of. I'm sick of this shit."

"I don't know what's going on exactly, but it's not fair to take it out on unsuspecting gardeners when your real problem seems to be with Michelle." Rudy shifted his feet. "I mean, what were you going to do? Ground that gardener for a week? I haven't seen you yell like that since Michelle ran away to my place when she was twelve."

"Rudy," Jerry said, spinning around. "It's nothing to do with my daughter, all right? It's that whole generation. They just want to garden because it's good for them, they don't care about the plants or the soil or feeding the community or any of that. It's a stress reliever. Gardening gets rid of toxins. Half of them are growing kale they'll never eat."

Rudy raised both of his hands and shook his head. "Enough. Whatever you have to tell yourself."

§

Jerry slammed the back door shut and scared the collie awake. The beagle came huffing into the kitchen. "Shut up," he snapped. The beagle wagged her tail and the collie whined uncertainly. He grabbed the house phone off the kitchen counter and punched in Michelle's number. Here he was thinking that he had raised someone different, when they all turned out the same, didn't they? And then they leave.

Michelle's voicemail box was full.

§

Four hours and six beers later, the peach tree lay in ruins, its limbs splayed out on the ground, its fruits neatly gathered in stacked boxes. Jerry pulled out his smartphone, went to the Facebook group page, and wrote: "Peach tree had to come down, unfortunately. The shade covered too many plots, it was too much fruit, and the branches were about to snap. There are plenty of peaches available, though. Come on by if you want to make some pies or do some canning!" He snapped a picture of the warm, fuzzy peaches resting peacefully in their boxes and posted that for good measure. He did not take a picture of the destroyed peach tree, of the surprising whiteness that hid behind its bark.

"We can clear the rest of this tomorrow," he said to Rudy. "Thanks for coming by."

Rudy nodded. "Mind if I take a box?"

Jerry shrugged. "Take your pick."

Rudy bent and hefted one of the pallet boxes onto his shoulders. It wasn't dark yet, but more crickets were singing, and the sky had taken on a rosy hue. Rudy looked into Jerry's eyes. "You are doing a good thing here, you know."

Jerry looked down at his beat-up tennis shoes and nodded. "Thank you."

"It doesn't matter why people garden, and you're always going to get a few jerks who don't participate. Don't take it so personally."

"Bye, Rudy."

"Okay. Have a good night now." Rudy turned and trudged up the hill, past plots overgrown with weeds, plots with scores of red tomatoes that had already burst in the sun, plots overrun by squash blossoms, his white shoes and socks gleaming in the fading light.

§

Later, Jerry sat on his porch and faced the garden. All four dogs lay together, ears pricked as they listened to the clinking sound the whiskey bottle made when he set it on the table. The cordless phone rested in the crook of his left arm and the smartphone sat on the windowsill. He listened to the birds and the whining of the mosquitos, drank in the dark smell of rain that would fall that night, and waited for the light to fade. He didn't look at the hole the peach tree had left.

One by one, the solar lights next to each garden plot came on like bright white fireflies, like a grid of stars.

DAVE MAINELLI
How to be a Man

DUSTIN DIDN'T THANK HIS FIVE-YEAR-OLD for grabbing a PBR out of the refrigerator and bringing it to him like he was told to. Why should he? Sons are supposed to do what their fathers tell them to do. It was how he was raised. It's how he would raise Jeffery. And as far as he was concerned, the little shit should be counting his lucky stars he was able to walk after pissing his bed again last night. It was at least the sixth time from his count. Karen said that morning it had to do with a leaky bladder, but he wasn't buying it.

He moved the ice pack up his back until he hit the right spot, and he let out a groan.

"You going to go see that chiropractor Jason told you about?" Karen asked as she picked up a few toys in the room. She threw them behind the sofa.

"Why would I hand over my hard-earned money to some bullshit witch doctor?"

"Because you're getting worse. You can barely get out of bed in the morning. And you heard what he said. He said the guy performed a miracle on him."

"Ahhgg." He waved her off. "We can't afford it. Plus, we ain't seen that asshole Jason since they went and bought a bigger house. Apparently, he and Michelle think they are better than us."

Karen mumbled her way into the kitchen. Something about Michelle still being her friend. Meanwhile, Jeffery had made his way back to the living room with his toy motorcycle. He wore only his Spider-Man underwear. His floppy blond hair and pale skin were almost as white as what was not painted on the briefs. He *vroomed* around the room with the motorcycle in the air and passed by Dustin a few times who searched through the guide on the television. He finally landed on a show about covering up bad tattoos called *Recover Ink*.

"Alright, keep it down, Jeffery. I'm trying to watch some TV now."

Jeffery circled in the room one more time.

"Jeffery!"

Jeffery turned, startled.

"Listen, boy!" Dustin pointed to his own ear.

Jeffery buzzed his way down the hall and back to his room as Dustin pushed up against his ice bag, put his feet up, and listened to a woman tell the tattoo artist her story of when she got an anchor on her shoulder after a drunken night out with her boyfriend. The anchor still screamed her boyfriend's name twelve years after they split. She cried into her hands as the tattoo artist rubbed her back. She told the camera it reminded her of that terrible relationship every day, and it caused problems with men in her life.

Dustin glanced down at the tattoo on the inside of his right arm. The letters USMC were faded black. He had one on his shoulder too. A skull-and-crossbones he had inked in El Paso one late night after drinking with his unit by an amateur at best. It was a night he would like to forget altogether. He'd like to forget the next day as well. That's when he woke up on the jail cell floor in his own vomit. If he could have that tattoo covered up, he would. He can't afford it.

"Pork chops okay, Dusty?" Karen called out from the kitchen.

Karen did an okay job of running the house as far as Dustin was concerned. She did fine with Jeffery too, although he seemed a little dumb for his age.

Dustin didn't understand why she held him back one more year from school. He felt it was so she could keep from working another year. A part-time job would be helpful. But they had fought over it so many times, and he usually ended up down at Teddy's getting shitfaced afterward, so he didn't bring it up anymore unless he was hellfire drunk and feeling downright surly.

"Yep."

"Green beans?"

"That's fine, Karen, Jesus. Do I ever say no? You don't have to ask every damn night."

"Yeah, well you whine about what I'm making all the time," she yelled from the kitchen. "Sorry if I want to make sure you're happy with what I'm making and all."

He could tell by the clarity of her voice she had necked out into the family room for the last line. He didn't turn to look at her. He wasn't going to do her the favor.

The tattoo artist stood at an artist's desk drawing out his sketch of the cover-up tattoo that would go over the anchor. It was an amazing version of a Bengal tiger's head. The woman receiving the new tattoo screamed in joy and broke down in tears when she saw it. She said it gave her strength and was how she wanted to feel about life—strong and fierce.

"Pffff," Dustin replied. "Whatever."

Karen's pop song ringtone went off in the kitchen, and she started loudly jabbering to one of her friends. The sound of her and her phone going off irritated him. They couldn't afford the damn iPhone, but she just had to have it. She always ran over their data limit. He laid into her last month about it. He told her if she had time to be texting and getting on Facebook all the time, she had time to be getting a damn job. She didn't take too well to that.

"Oh, I know," she said so the whole house could hear. "I couldn't believe that!"

Dustin leaned back and shouted upward, over, and backwards into the air. "Can you keep it down? Trying to watch a show in here!" He grunted and snorted too, for good measure.

Karen's voice lowered, but he could still hear her say, "Something is up Dusty's butt."

"'Bout to shove something up your butt," he mumbled.

The night he got the tattoo they went to a few strip clubs on Gateway Boulevard West. There was a whole slew of them. Dusty and his guys were letting off some steam. When they hit Tequila Sunrise, Dusty was a mess. His tattoo was burning, and he had downed enough Jack Daniels for the squad. The trouble happened when a gal named Mindy and he went to the back room for a private dance. Their bouncers didn't stand a chance against his unit. But the police were called. And he was dishonorably discharged after the process ran its course.

Back to the show: the woman now lay in the chair getting her tiger tattoo. She was facedown and wore a tube top, of sorts, around her waist. The show interchanged between interviewing the tattoo artist and the woman and showing him applying the tattoo.

The tattoo artist said, "I don't just take away bad tattoos. That's not how I see it. This woman has a memory of something she doesn't want in her life anymore. It was a bad relationship. And I have a feeling it was maybe worse than we are being told. I am removing a stain from her life and giving her the gift of beautiful art; art which she can see every day and can hopefully motivate her to go out there and be whatever she wants to be. I truly believe that. This tiger could change her life."

Dustin scanned the room, desperately wanting to share his disgust. "Are you fucking kidding me?"

The show went to a commercial. He pushed the ice pack up on his back.

Dustin had to be reminded of that night and being discharged every time he looked at that tattoo. Usually in the morning as he got dressed. He was reminded of it again now. He finished his beer.

"Hey, Jeffery! Get your ass out here!"

Karen leaned out of the kitchen again. The smell and the sound of the pork chops sizzling in the pan were both prevalent. "What do you need Dusty, a beer?"

"Yeah."

"Well, I will get it for you."

Jeffery never appeared. That bothered Dustin. He should've come running when he was called. Kids today had no respect. Karen handed him his beer, and he swapped her his empty with her hardly taking notice of him.

"Who you talking to anyway?" he said, as he snapped the can open. "And do we have any whiskey?"

She flinched and shot a glare at him. "Jennifer, if you need to know." She continued in a softer voice as if he still couldn't hear her. "Can you believe him? I know. He wants whiskey now, too. He's going to be awful later."

He liked being the bad guy. He did the work. He made the money. Maybe it wasn't a lot, but it was all they had. "When's dinner gonna be ready?"

"Soon. Be patient. Jesus."

"I work all goddamn day while you sit around here doing God-knows-what. Dinner should be ready!"

"Okay. I was busy."

"Doing what?"

"I was doing laundry and had to go to the store and stuff."

Dustin mumbled into his beer, "Had all day to get that stuff done."

He took a drink from his beer and set it down. She handed him his shot of whiskey without looking at him, and he downed it in one gulp. The show came back on with the woman in wraps waiting for the big reveal. That's when he noticed Jeffrey a couple feet away, staring at him.

"What the hell do you want?"

Jeffery shrugged.

"Now tell me something. Why is it you go around in your skivvies all the time, huh? Aren't you a little old to be running around like that?"

Jeffery examined his underpants then raised his look back to Dustin. He shrugged.

"Don't you talk anymore?"

"Yeah."

"How come you don't do what I tell you to?"

He shrugged again.

"Jesus H. Christ, boy. When I was your age, I would've gotten my ass whooped if I didn't do what I was told."

Jeffery stood frozen, motorcycle still in his hand.

"And why aren't you outside running around with other boys playing and getting into shit? When I was your age, they had to drag me in for dinner. I used to get yelled at for being late."

Jeffery shrugged. His chin dropped to his sternum.

The call finally came from the kitchen. "Dinner!"

He turned Jeffery around and pointed him towards the hallway.

"Now go on and put on some clothes for dinner. And do as I tell ya. You're gonna learn to be a man."

Jeffery ran to his room. When Dustin turned around, the finished tattoo was being shown from every angle on the woman. It was impressive. A past reminder of something bad turned into something amazing. A second chance. The woman smiled ear to ear. She couldn't stop hugging the artist. Dustin shook his head as he slowly stood up from his chair. He set the ice bag on the table. Condensation covered the bag, and it left a puddle on the table. He limped to the kitchen.

"You want milk or a beer?" Karen asked without turning around.

"What do you think?"

"Sit down. I'll get you a plate."

"How was work today?"

"I'm a plumber. I unclogged three shitty toilets and had to replace a twenty-five-year-old restaurant garbage disposal. How was yours?"

Karen pursed her lips. "I am trying to be nice. You don't have to be such an asshole." She turned and yelled, "Jeffery! Dinner!"

"I told him to put some damn clothes on before dinner."

"Why would you do that?"

"What do you mean, why?"

They stared each other down.

Karen set a plate of bread down. She put her hand on her hip like a waitress from a seventies sitcom. "Yes. Why? So, he can get clean clothes dirty for no reason before bed?"

"What in the . . . What is going on in this house? So, we just eat in our skivvies around here now? Is that how it is then?"

Dustin stood up and clumsily took his pants off. Karen put her hand to her mouth with a grin behind it. He flung the pants over by the refrigerator in a pile. His white underwear, spotted and with holes in the band, shone like a light against his blue flannel shirt and peach legs. Karen's giggle grew louder. Dustin began to chuckle as well and took the joke even further and took off his shirt. He unbuttoned his flannel until he stood only in his briefs and socks. They both laughed as he danced around like a fool.

"I piss myself," Dustin said in a mocking tone, doing a type of dance with his arms and legs bent.

Karen turned to fix a plate, still laughing, when she noticed Jeffery in the doorway to the kitchen. Dustin realized Karen had stopped laughing and turned also. Jeffery stood barefoot with his blue pajama bottoms and a white T-shirt on. His curly, blond locks hung over his freshly red-lined eyes which now barely held his newly formed tears. His expression was more of shock. With a flash, he turned and ran back to his room. A large bang from his bedroom door slamming shut filled the house. Karen went after him.

Dustin shrugged and sat down. He drank from his beer and started on his dinner.

AMBER MAY
The Empty Seats

THE CARDS STICK TOGETHER as Uncle Joe shuffles the deck. He has a toothpick sticking from his lips, working it around in his mouth with his tongue.

I try to discreetly check my notifications, but a nudge from my mother next to me puts a stop to it.

"Aren't you having fun, Bryan?" Mom asks.

"Sure," I say. I think back to my paused video game in my room. I was hiding there before my brother dragged me out to play UNO with the rest of the family. It's apparently a tradition now since we played it last year.

Mom goes back to her conversation with my brother as Uncle Joe finally deals. Everyone quiets down as we organize our cards. Uncle Joe flips the first card over, and Aunt Trish lays down a green Skip. I set my deck face down on the table and try to wait patiently as everyone else goes.

Grandma plays a red nine on a green six and the table erupts with objections. Grandma takes her card back, flapping her arm around slightly and then placing a new one down. "It's so hard to tell them apart," she says.

"It's okay, we all know you learned it from Grandpa," my brother teases.

It's quiet for a moment as everyone looks down at the table, smiling to themselves. I watch as Grandma takes a sip of water and stares at her ring for a moment. Uncle Joe takes his turn.

"He used to yell at us when we'd try and correct him," Mom laughs after a beat.

I place a red Draw Two onto the pile.

"He'd get so angry," Aunt Trish says, smiling, jerking with repressed laugher.

"God, he hated this game," says Grandma. The whole table laughs. I place another card onto the pile.

"You know who loved that game though? Dave loved this game," Uncle Joe says. "Bryan, remember when we went hunting that one time and we tried to play UNO in the hunting blind?"

"And then you got pissed that you lost and threw the cards? Yeah," I say, laughing along with the rest of the table.

"And then you shot that turkey," Uncle Joe continues. "And you got it in one shot. Remember how you used to tease Dave about it? 'How many shots did it take you?' you'd say, 'Six? It took me one!'" The whole table nods their heads in remembrance, grinning to themselves.

"He would never take me hunting after that," I say, laying down another card. That's not true. I had decided I liked video games instead of hunting, feeling out of place with Uncle Joe and his lifelong hunting buddy. That trip was the first and only one I had ever gone on.

"He loved hunting," Uncle Joe says to the table; it sounds like *I miss you*.

Mom clears her throat, "I remember when we used to play this game at Great Grandma Irene's place."

"I remember that too," Aunt Trish says. "Once, I played a game with her, and I had a handful of Draw Twos. I just kept giving them to her," she pauses, laughing to herself as she sets a card down. "By the fifth time I did it, the whole table was howling at the look on her face! Then she quietly looked over at me and said, 'Aren't you a bitch?'"

"That was the only time I ever heard her curse," Mom says between giggles.

After the laughter dies out, I say, "I don't remember ever playing UNO with Grandma Irene."

I say it at a more reasonable level, quieting the loud volume at the table. I start to pull out the next card I want to play, but Aunt Trish changes the color. I slot the card back into its place and play a different one.

Mom hums, nodding, "She got really bad arthritis and wasn't able to play towards the end."

My brother sets a card down and then straightens the discard pile, Grandma almost knocking into him in her eagerness to place her card. She snatches her hand back last second, so they won't collide.

I suck in a breath, "I remember playing in a kiddie pool all the time at Grandma Irene's."

"Yeah, I remember that," my brother says. "We refused to play in it at first, I think?"

I laugh. "Yeah, it was pink, and we thought we were too cool for pink."

"I remember her getting it," Aunt Trish says. "She found it in the clearance section with a big hole in it. She patched it up, somehow."

"Actually, Larry had fixed it," says Grandma. She's frowning at her ring.

"Dad was always fixing everything for her," whispers Mom. She's not laughing anymore and not looking anyone in the eye. There's a lot of eye-contact avoiding going around the table though, so only I notice.

"He was always fixing everything around here too," Grandma says. She's swaying back and forth slightly in her chair. "Now that he's not here, I don't know—everything is—" her voice breaks, cutting her off. She shakes her head to herself and stares determinedly at the table.

Everyone is quiet again. I clear my throat. "UNO."

DAVID McCLEERY
The Drowned

WHEN WINTER CAME, MY YOUNGER Brother Ian and I would go out to the farm pond far off in the barren fields and fish with only the moon and stars to light our work. We spoke in whispers when we spoke at all, not to each other, but to ourselves, or perhaps to the silver-coated coyotes who came and waited at the edge of their shadows for the small silver, flashing fish we'd leave behind.

And on one night when the moon was full, because we only fished when the moon was full, we made our way across the ice. Ian carried his thin coat over his shoulder because it was warm, because all week the weather had felt like March.

We were two moon shadows, but we were not weightless, not like the fish in the frozen pond, the thin bands of clouds, or the one owl that waited in the cedar tree wooing his slow warning. And as we walked over the thin ice, fog descended.

There are holes in the ice, holes in our lives, our days, nights, and our dreams. There are holes that open up and take us down, holes that swallow us like mouths and consume us. *Take my hand, young Brother. Take my warm hand, and I will help you. Grab onto my life, and I shall try and save you. I will pull you from the mouth of your death. I will not allow you to sink down into that cold loneliness.* But he was behind me, twenty feet behind, and silent and slow like the fog.

Warmth, winter, ice, two boys, and an owl watchful in the woods, the moon up and bright through the shroud of fog. I should have been the one to step. Not him. Not Ian. I should have been the cold winter angel.

I heard the ice break, and when I turned he was gone, with only that crack to announce his departure. *Take my hand, young Brother, and I will lead you across to the safety of the morning. Take my hand, and I will carry you out of your death and set you down in a warm bed. Let me lean down into that dark hole and grab you back.*

I ran to where he should have been, but nothing, only the water lapping the edge of an ice hole we'd cut weeks before. I fell to my knees, called his name. I called into that ink-black water and frantically spread the water with my hands, making an opening for him to reappear, to rise again into his life.

Never was there a hole so dark and bottomless as that. Even now I can feel the cold water against my forearms and hands, and I gasp for breath. I can feel the growing numbness in my hands' futile search, in their senseless, numb, unfeeling search. I plied the waters and thought once I had hold of him. I felt soft flesh under my grip only to discover, in fright and despair, my own cold arm clutched in my hand. How long I reached into that icy water, I do not know.

Eventually, I stopped. I sat on the ice, and as I did, the white owl floated silently out of the fog. With wings spread wide, the owl glided straight toward me, then swooped down so close I felt the great bird pass over. I watched as the owl soared into a treetop on the other side of the pond, and when I looked down there, in the hole, was my Brother.

His red-checkered shirt floated there and plugged the hole. I pushed him under with my foot until his arms drifted up into the rough opening, and I took hold and struggled to pull him free of the pond. He just fit through the narrow opening. I slid him up on the ice and turned him over. I hovered over him. His hair was quickly turning to ice. I peered into his glassy eyes and spoke to him, slapped his cheeks. I remember thinking if I could just put his eyes in my mouth, I might warm his smile back into them. If I could take his blue lips and tongue into my own mouth, I might dissolve the death. I wanted to warm his ears and nose in my hands and place them back on his face.

He was gone, but I could not leave him there, not with the coyotes about. So, I tied my scarf around his left wrist, and I began to pull him, to slide him back across the ice to the bank of the pond. I drug his dead weight, and like some poor, faded star, he fell across the face of that pond under the white moon to the edge where the coyotes patiently waited.

He lay on his back. I tried, but he was too heavy to lift. I could not carry him home, and I could not leave him there. So, I did what I had to do. I took his belt and lashed his two wrists to the center of a large branch and pulled him back across the ice. Then under the watchful eye of the owl, I slid him feet first back into his death like a fish released back into its life. How easily he went back to his bed, how effortlessly the water swallowed him up, how quickly he remembered what he had to do. He floated in the ice hole, hanging from his hands which were supported by the branch that spanned the hole. He would never drift away from me again.

Father rose from his chair when I came into the house. Mother too. His arms were outstretched, and his palms were turned upward as if he expected me to hand him something, as if he were ready to take on what I had carried those three miles and carry to this day. I held out my Brother's death, and he took it in his arms.

"Oh, my son," he said. "Oh, my son what has happened?" he asked, briefly touching my frozen shirt. Mother began to cry and took my frostbitten hands into her own, hands of which two fingers would soon disappear. They had touched my Brother's death and had to be cut away. Look, see the two fingers gone. I hold out my right hand and make the sign of my Brother's death.

I led Father out into the cold night. Mother refused to go. He followed, allowed me to guide him back to his young son as if he could not, or would not, find his own way to that death. Twice I had to stop and allow him to catch up, waited for him to place his hand on my shoulder, nudge me gently with his hand, asking me to continue on for him.

We walked through the fields filled with fog until we came to the edge of the frozen pond. I looked out over the ice and could see that the owl had gone, the coyotes too. Father stepped out first, and the ice groaned under him.

"Stop," I called.

"Yes," he said, "you go."

So, I ventured out and walked toward where my Brother floated in the one-eyed pond under the sleeping moon. I took hold of the branch he hung from, and the moon slipped from under a thin lid of cloud, peeked out and down. The February moon had to see, had to have a look after all.

I again pulled my Brother from that dangerous hole. He lay silent on the ice. He was a stranger to me then, all purple and thick, someone I did not recognize in death. I wanted to unbind him and let him slip back under. Allow the ice hole to heal him, seal him up.

But I drug Ian back to the edge of the pond where Father waited. He dropped to one knee, became a hunter examining a carcass. He looked at the neck, the arms. He ran his hand across Ian's jaw. There was little sadness, only wonder, amazement, disbelief.

My hands were aching, and I began to shiver. Father looked up, and perhaps I said something, I don't remember. What would I have said? That I thought the ice would hold? That I had forgotten the thin hole and not warned Ian? That I should have been the one to step off?

Oh, my Brother, what has become of you? What has happened to your small body? To your sweet breath? What hand has turned you cold and still? Have you gone off into the stillness that hides in the night, that distant silence that lies in the darkness between the stars, the silence the lies between each breath?

I dropped down beside Father and gasped for breath. "Stop," Father said. "Just stop. Not here. Get a hold of yourself. We have to get your Brother home."

He stood and reached down and lifted my Brother from the bed of snow he had found for himself. Father set this great grief across his broad back and began to walk steadily home.

I followed. I turned around, and behind me I could see the owl perched like a white angel in the darkness of the cedar tree.

We walked down the stubbled cornrows, half full of snow. The night suddenly cleared of fog and the moon lay bright, and I became colder than I had ever been. I walked slowly and began to get sleepy. I wanted nothing more than to lie down and sleep in the gray-white shadows of snow. Twice I sat and told Father I could go no farther. And twice he stopped and said without turning, that he could bear only one dead son, that I had to keep going, that the house was not far. He said he didn't want to have to come back and fetch another.

So, I struggled to my feet and followed, kept walking until we arrived back home. We came up behind the barn and the dogs tromped over to us, and Father carried Ian up the steps past Mother and into the warm kitchen. He lay him on the floor and struggled to remove Ian's boots. Then he sat on the cold, wet floor, as Mother wept. It was then I first saw my Father go under. Quietly, slowly, gradually, as one enters sleep, I saw him sink.

I too have struggled to stay above the surface of that grief. Especially when there are skaters on a pond on a winter night. I watch the figures move across the ice like shadows circling soundlessly but for the whir of their skates, the breath of their blades on ice. I watch the couples join hands and dance away into the frigid shadows, and my heart begins to race, and a tightness comes across my chest. I start to gasp for breath. But then I pull myself out, take a deep breath, let flow one deep sanctified breath out into the cold moonlight for him, for Ian.

JIM PLATH
In Block Letters

ADAM AND I MET IN high school. I was new to town and he was alone, so he invited me to sit with him at the lunch table. I'd say we saved each other from awkward solitude, but even then, I knew only I would've been bothered by that. He spent his teen years in the coat closets of the world, and he counted himself lucky for the quietude. I saw it in the way he dressed, simple in unremarkable, patternless clothing too plain to belong to any style or era. Sometimes he'd sketch iconic characters on his white sneakers in blue pen, and that was as close as I ever saw him come to making a display of himself.

We bonded over classic science fiction. He loved the philosophy of it all, the symbolism and the observations about human nature. I liked trying to piece together the threads of science and trying to imagine how the things in those stories could become reality. We were geeks in the days before that went mainstream. I played it down, but Adam always carried an armload of comic books to read in study hall, and he ignored anyone who found it funny.

On the downslope of my thirties, my marriage fell apart, and Adam saved me from loneliness again. I never knew why, but Adam and my wife didn't like one another. He never said so himself. He just stopped visiting once we moved across the state line. I assumed she'd said something to upset him, because if it'd been the reverse, she'd have told me.

We'd stayed in touch the way people do these days, but ten years put some gray in my beard since I'd last seen him in person. He offered me the spare room in his apartment for whatever part of the rent I could cover. Adam never kept pictures of himself or posted any online, so it surprised me to see how little he'd changed. His build remained lanky, and his hair retained all its deep brown with only the suggestion of thinning at the corners of his forehead. He still dressed like someone about to work in a garden.

What didn't surprise me was the place where he lived, grand or simple, depending on the vantage point. From a distance, The Old Town Mill Apartments building impressed with its towering redbrick façade and high-arched windows. A stone walkway led to a set of white pilasters at the front entrance. Behind the property, a narrow creek stroked its banks with slow water, brushing close to the building in the suggestion of a moat before carrying on toward a curtain of leafless trees.

The impression fell apart at close range. The stones in the walkway wore flat and cracked, showing tufts of dead grass in the network of open wounds. At the entrance, the white pilasters shed paint in quarter-sized scabs that piled to either side and waited to be cleared. Inside, the lobby carried the biting stench of cosmetic astringent, and the hallways smelled like locker rooms washed in aftershave to mask the odor. The aesthetic of the apartment itself made it Adam's; the secondhand furniture, mismatched drapes, and frameless movie posters hung with pushpins to the living room walls. To Adam, only a few things mattered, and most of them didn't matter much.

At the end of my first week living there, I decided to contribute by doing some grocery shopping. Later, I opened the refrigerator and found most of what I'd bought moved to one side of the shelves with duplicate items of other brands on the opposite end. I found him in his room, sitting upright in bed with a tablet in his lap, and I asked him about it.

"Is something wrong?" I asked. "I mean with the stuff I bought. I noticed you went and did more shopping."

He looked up, mouth wide open as though he'd bitten into something too hot to swallow, but he didn't answer.

I went on. "I just hope you don't think I bought that stuff just for me. I mean, you're welcome to it."

"Not to be a jerk . . ." He put the tablet to the side and swung his legs over the edge of the bed. "It's just I'm fussy about brands I buy, companies I do business with. Things like that."

"Oh," I said as I looked around his room, noted the austerity of it, the unpainted wood bed frame he may have built himself, the shelves empty but for a trio of library books. "I'm sorry. I didn't realize that."

"I try not to preach. It's an imperfect system anyway." He gave a nervous laugh, gestured toward the tablet on his bed and patted the rectangular bulge that formed the outline of his cell phone in the hip pocket of his jeans. "Sometimes you've got to dance with the devil."

"I can double check the brands I buy next time if you want me to. Do you have, like, a list or something?"

"Something," he said and took a breath before standing. He reached back and pulled a green, palm-sized notepad from his back pocket. "I do a lot of research, follow business news, track what company's buying what smaller company."

He handed me the notepad, and I began to read it until I realized he'd filled most of the pages, spelled out the names of parent companies in block letters at the top, drawn branches down to clusters of subsidiaries with numbered footnotes on his grievances with them below. I remembered him taking notes in history class when we were kids, line after line of scribbled half sentences until he got to something that interested him, Washington and the Whiskey Rebellion, Prophetstown and Tenskwatawa. Things he wanted to read more about later were written in big block letters. I didn't finish flipping the pages of his notepad before handing it back to him.

"Most people don't realize it," he started again, his voice a little higher. "They hear about the owner of some fast food chain who does something they don't like, they think they'll just boycott that chain. They don't realize a bigger company owns it." After a pause, he added a nervous laugh. "I realize I look like I've lost my mind."

Only when my tongue began to dry did I realize I'd been staring, mouth agape. "No," I answered with a smile. "You just took me back to high school for a second. I know this stuff matters to you because I can actually read it."

"No one really thinks boycotting a frozen food company means caring what type of motor oil you use, but it does. No company is just one entity anymore."

"I guess you're right. I really don't pay that much attention."

"Most people don't," he assured me. "And that's cool. I don't expect them to, really. I don't even have a 401k."

"Seriously?" Only after the question escaped my lips did I realize I'd spat it more than spoken it. When we were in college, Adam ran afoul of a film professor who assigned a paper on the technical significance of D.W. Griffith's racist epic, *The Birth of a Nation*. I think I just always assumed the life expectancy of idealism to be a maximum of twenty-nine years. I nodded my admiration and added, "You are hardcore."

"Well, I can't find anyone to manage it who will assure me I won't be invested in companies that run sweatshops or sell lead-painted toys to kids, so I just don't invest."

When he sang at my wedding reception, I learned Adam had been playing piano since he was six-years-old. A few years later, I learned he spoke Czech and translated the newspaper for his grandmother almost every morning. I always wanted my answer to those revelations to be that he didn't volunteer much about himself, but just then, as he tucked his notepad away, I saw him smile. A fragile curl in his lip followed a twitch of his eye, and I understood he took pride in the effort that notepad recorded. I blamed myself for everything I took too long to learn about my friend.

If I ever entertained the idea that I could live Adam's lifestyle, or that I really wanted to, it didn't last beyond that conversation in his room. If that disappointed him, he didn't show it. Months passed, and I usually let him do the shopping, chipping in with some cash instead of doing the legwork. When I did buy something that didn't fit his list, he just moved it aside in the cupboard or fridge.

The only time the issue came up again for discussion was on a Friday night when he'd invited some of his work friends over to the apartment. My job kept me late that night, so I picked up the mail in the lobby and joined the party long in progress. I found them all three-quarters through Adam's nineties' alternative rock playlist, but they kept the music low. In the far corner of the living room, by the sun-faded *Blade Runner* poster, two ladies took turns balancing small stacks of quarters on their elbows and catching them. Adam sat on the sofa in front of a half-empty bowl of chips, speaking louder than he meant to with a bulky frog-eyed man standing in the kitchen. Everyone was drunk, the kind of drunk people get in their thirties. No one would pass out. They'd just take too long to say things their sober selves wouldn't say at all.

From the context of the conversation, I gathered Adam had been asked why we had two types of orange juice. I nodded at our guests without entering the discussion and handed Adam his piece of mail. It looked official. Adam didn't wait to open it. His face fell as he read.

"Something wrong?" I asked.

Adam didn't answer at first. He called over across the divide into the kitchen to the frog-eyed man. "Would you grab me that red pen in the jar on the counter?"

He brought him the pen and Adam looked up at me from the sofa. "It's fine. They're selling the building is all."

"To who?" I asked.

"Someone I'm not crazy about," he muttered.

One of the ladies chirped from behind, "How do you score that in your book?"

Adam didn't answer. He pulled his green notepad from his pocket and flipped to the back, a section I stopped short of when he'd shown me the pad before. There, a column of red ink marked the last page, a list of payments he couldn't avoid making to companies he disliked or knew too little about, as he put it, the devils he danced with. There, below the balance of his car loan and the cost of his smartphone, he wrote out the monthly rent in block letters, circled it and ignored anyone who found it funny.

JIM PLATH
Silver Dancer

THERE'S AN ICE CREAM PARLOR on Twelfth Street. The floor is a black and white checkerboard and the walls are rounded with booths upholstered in overstuffed red vinyl. It's made to look old, and a retro-model jukebox in the corner plays standards from the fifties and sixties to make it sound that way. The people inside are anachronisms, twenty-somethings on tablets and laptops, a patchwork of trilbies, knee-high socks, and suspenders over T-shirts. There's also Josh.

If an average man were to lie in a leaf pile, Josh might be the imprint left behind. His hair is long because he doesn't care to cut it. He's thin because he forgets to eat between work and school, and he's out of shape because he sleeps his free time away. Josh lives alone across the street, above a bar and grill, in a small apartment that smells like old corn oil. Most weeknights he crosses over to use the parlor's free Wi-Fi for research and homework. It takes him longer than it should because the day's headlines and op-ed pieces flood his browser and he must know the score in the world. On a particular Wednesday, he sits with his laptop at the counter listening to The Kingston

Trio and reading about a house fire in Phoenix that killed a young family of four. Josh's jaw cramps as he grits his teeth combing through the comments on the article, anonymous users betting the blame away on immigrant contractors or imported products from China. Beside him, a plastic spoon sinks into a paper cup where chocolate ice cream warms to tepid mud.

The manager stands behind the counter. He doesn't mind that Josh isn't eating and won't order more, because it's only Wednesday and the place isn't half full. There's a lull between songs before Jim Croce's opening notes to "Rapid Roy (That Stock Car Boy)" shriek through the speakers. Before the vocals start, he hears Josh mutter something without losing focus on his laptop, the open monitor hides half his face like the cardboard flap of a child's box fort.

Josh doesn't mean to be heard, but when the manager asks him to repeat himself, he can't think of a polite way not to. "I just said this one's from the seventies." He waits before he adds, "The song, I mean. It's from the seventies."

The manager frowns and asks, "Is that a problem?"

"No, it's just different. I think everything else I've heard is from before then."

He lowers his balding head toward Josh's laptop. "I didn't realize you were so wrapped up in the atmosphere."

Josh's lips part and hold silent before he finds the words he wants to use. "I didn't mean to be a snot about it."

"It's funny," the manager starts without acknowledging the apology. "I'm sure you're right about the year of the song, but it sounds like it could be from the fifties, doesn't it?"

"I'm sorry?"

"I wasn't around back then." He brushes his fingers across the slick part of his bare scalp. "Don't let this fool you, that was way before my time, but you still have an idea of what it sounded like, you know? Like, I don't speak a word of Japanese, but I know when something sounds like Japanese, right?"

Josh lets his eyes linger on the manager, waiting for a moment to pass where he can get back to his laptop. "I can't argue with that."

"Just a thought," the manager replies. "Sometimes you just have to enjoy the moment." He raises a finger toward the area behind Josh where the checkerboard floor is open between the booths and the counter. "Like this guy."

Josh turns his torso to see behind himself. There's a man dancing a sort of twist that becomes a shuffle at the end of the song's verse. He might be in his eighties. His hair is thick and white, but the light crawls across it like polished silver. He wears a pinstripe vest over a crimson shirt. Josh thinks he must have come in after him, and he watches the man dance through the rest of the guitar solo. There's a wild spin and the old man is up on one leg. Josh thinks his hip can't take all his weight, and his stomach throbs while he thinks about having to catch the man when he falls, but that never happens.

The song ends, and the man approaches a young lady in the corner with his hand extended toward her. Only when the man stands still does his face show the faults and valleys in his skin. Josh thinks they must be deepening, and the old man will come apart with one more sudden move. The young lady smiles and says something in too soft a voice for Josh to hear, then she gestures to a young man at her side. The old man puts his free hand on his heart and announces, "I'll dance with him next, I promise."

That's what happens. The young lady joins the old man on the floor for a song, then as promised, as the music calms, he shares a slow dance with her boyfriend, punctuated with a dip at the end as the room applauds and laughs. Josh thinks the man will stop, or take a break, and he returns to his article about the Arizona house fire because he has a paper coming due. It's a history paper about the Austro-Hungarian Empire, but he can't think about that until he knows how that fire started and why no one could escape the house. Another song ends and the small crowd claps again. Someone at the end of the counter whistles their praise, and Josh knows the old man must still be dancing. He stares at his monitor without reading.

Josh next looks up from his laptop just as the old man is getting ready to leave. His hair is slick then, and beads of sweat trace runways at his temples, but he smiles so widely his cheeks press his eyes closed as he moves toward the door. Some voice floats out across the room and calls him Silver Dancer. He waves as the door shuts behind him. The room holds some trace of him. Young couples meet on the floor for dull-footed impressions of what they'd seen. The night waits for closing time to die.

§

More Wednesdays pass, and the Silver Dancer comes for every one of them. The crowds start growing for Wednesday nights, and they aren't just twenty-somethings in ironic T-shirts anymore. The Silver Dancer gives a brief tap lesson to a middle-aged man in khakis. He hunches forward and invites a six-year-old girl to stand on his toes for a dance. The manager starts calling the dancer his mascot, and he pays him with a free milkshake.

Through the tin clatter of old guitars, Josh reads articles about a bullying victim in Toledo and an increase in methamphetamine addiction in Prague. The place doesn't feel empty enough on Wednesdays anymore, so now he lets a large cup of chocolate ice cream sour on the counter at his side. He finishes reading a blog post about internet privacy, but he's only halfway through a write-up on his biology lab results when he feels the sting of cold liquid seeping through his shirt sleeve. He manages to jerk his arm back without tipping his cup over, but his sweatshirt is a dull yellow that hides none of the chocolate stain on the elbow.

"I don't know if the stain will come out," a voice pours in as the music softens and dies. "But this'll dry you off, at least."

Josh turns to find the old man, the Silver Dancer, approaching with a handful of napkins. He smiles and works the paper to his sleeve. "Thank you."

He points to Josh's laptop. "Interesting reading?"

"It's an assignment, actually."

He laughs. "That doesn't mean it can't be interesting."

Josh folds a napkin over and holds it in place to the brown spot on his elbow. "I guess you're right about that."

"Kid, I see you in here every week. All the time, you've got that computer in front of you. I've got to think you're enjoying yourself."

"It's not all just assignments." Josh pulls the napkin from his elbow and decides the paper has absorbed as much of the stain as it's going to. "I take breaks, read news articles and stuff."

The old man laughs again. "You got school work to do, that's got to get done. I get it, but you read the news for a break? You'll drive yourself nuts living that way, trust me on that."

"Not knowing about bad things doesn't make them go away."

"Neither does sitting in front of a screen. Don't let it grind you down, kid."

Josh nods, but he doesn't answer.

"Bad things happen all over. If I was there, I'd try to help. If they were here," he looks around the room, "I'd ask them to dance."

The two part company, and Josh finishes his assignment before the parlor closes that night. Weeks pass, and it becomes a rhythm. He continues crossing the street to use the Wi-Fi on weeknights, and he continues to see the old man dance with strangers on Wednesdays until the weather turns cold and rain leaves an ice veneer on the sidewalks after sundown. In the first few weeks without the Silver Dancer, people still come out in force on Wednesdays. They wonder aloud if anyone's seen him, and they decide the weather's keeping him at home. After a month, people stop asking. Wednesdays leave the parlor half empty again, and Josh goes back to ordering a small cup to sit with. Wednesday nights die faster now.

§

Between semesters, Josh takes a drive into the country. He stops at a gas station off the interstate, on a scrap of underdeveloped land at the meeting point between two suburbs. White Christmas lights make solid rings around the windows, but the neon lights that sell beer and lotto tickets flicker like the wings of a half-dead housefly. There's a middle-aged woman behind the counter with her hair pulled back. She's humming along to classical music crackling through a radio speaker, but the corners of her mouth are downturned, and her eyes are sunken and still. Josh pays her for the fuel he's pumped and for a single rose wrapped in clear plastic in a bin beside the register.

"They're not real," she says. "Just so you know. They're some kind of fabric made to look like flowers."

"That's okay," Josh answers. "Sometimes it's enough to make it feel right anyway."

She hands him the imitation flower, and Josh passes it back to her.

"Something wrong?"

"It's for you," he answers.

"What for?"

Josh wants to tell her a story, but he doesn't know how to tell it. Instead, he sighs and shrugs. "Because I don't know how to dance."

ELIZABETH POTTER
Seeing Red

"YOU'RE GOING TO HELL"

Today in school we're learning about the marks that come at the end of sentences, but I don't know how to write an end mark for the smile that ends that one. It's not a question mark. Everyone who isn't in the family pictures I color and put on the fridge is going to hell. I love all the eighteen sisters and brothers in those pictures, ten more than how old I am. I love them even more than I love the Bible. But I can't tell Gramps that. If I did, his face would crumple the way he crumpled my drawing of Jesus loving everyone that he stomped on when I showed it to him. He says God doesn't love everyone and that we're supposed to love the Bible more than everything under . . .

"Elijah, when do you use an exclamation mark?"

My teacher snaps my attention back into my chair at school, and I snap back at her, "You're going to hell!"

That's just the right ending for that sentence, an exclamation mark. Teacher doesn't like that answer even though it's right, and she pulls me by the arm to the back of the class.

"Elijah. You can't say things like that to me. Or to anyone. What you say at home is one thing, but at school you have to watch your words."

"But it's the truth. To not say the truth is a sin."

"Being kind and making friends isn't a sin. Don't you want to make friends?"

"I can't be friends with people who are going to hell."

Teacher is not happy with that answer, but she lets it go, lets me go, and lets her face fall back into a fake sort of smile. It looks like the paper bag mask I made in crafts yesterday. I really wish I could wear that mask here at school. Then maybe I wouldn't have to shrivel up like my toes do when I can't find the bravery to get out of the bath and step onto cold tiles. There's lots and lots of cold tile at school. I know it as well as I know the scabs on my knees. That's because when you shrivel up, you can't look up. Not that I want to look up. Up is where all the looks of other kids are that make me feel like a leopard. Like the people in the Bible who were spotty with sores and shiny with blisters. Nobody but Jesus would touch those people, and no one at school will touch me except to shove me.

Mom and Dad would not smile if they saw how I shrivel at school. When we aren't waving signs, my brothers and sisters and I are supposed to be signs. Walking words of God. I tried that at school for awhile, but I got food spilled all over me and my head smashed into a toilet bowl. After that, I tried playing sick for a week, but Mom caught on. She was almost as mad as Gramps is when he lets out his bee laugh that buzzes in your ears and makes you do whatever he wants without even knowing. Mom was mad because I lied to her, and God does not love liars. But she doesn't know how much I love being sick. When I'm sick is the only time she's all mine and makes everything about me. Chicken soup, my favorite Bible stories read snuggled up to her side, and her voice singing me to sleep are the closest things I can think of to heaven. That and being swarmed by my brothers and sisters. Every day after school, they swarm me and show me how those leopard people must have felt when Jesus touched them.

Today they buzz around me with Bible verses all the way to Tenth Street, which is where my whole family is most days we aren't at a fag-lover's funeral in another city. Today I'm holding a sign that says, "Pray for More Dead Kids!" I really like this sign because I'm a kid, but I'll never die because I obey

God. I also like it because it's got lots of green on it like a turtle. It's really sad that turtles don't get to swim up to heaven, but God doesn't open up his gate to animals. That's why we aren't allowed to have pets. So, I pretend that all of our signs are our pets, and we have an entire zoo of them. "Thank God for 9/11" is very floppy and reminds me of a bird trying to fly away. "You Eat Your Kids," I growl mean and mad like a bear with an empty belly when I hold it. "AIDs Cures Gays" has a really long stick attached to it like the neck of a giraffe.

I'm thinking about all of our sign-pets when a car stops right in front of me, and a big man gets out with the face of a cinnamon bear. It's all red and mashed up like someone chewed on him for a bit and then spit him out. He spits the sentence, "If you aren't one of those dead kids soon, I'll kill you myself, you Bible-thumping bastard." I start shaking and wipe off the spit, but when I can see again, I'm no longer scared for me.

A few steps from me, Daddy is on the ground squished beneath the cinnamon-bear man. For a second, I think this man is actually a bear or one of those people who eat other people as he attacks my daddy. Daddy just lays with no fight in him and with blood smeared all over his face, making him redder than the man hitting him. He looks like the cinnamon-bear man's last word before he drives away in his car, "Jesus." But he's not Jesus. He's my daddy, and there's no way Jesus or God did this to him. But Daddy disagrees.

When I was the number of fingers on one hand, my sister Joanna got hit by a car. Joanna, who can always pull laughs out of pouts, got hit by a car and the words, "That's from God, you hateful bitch!" And it was according to Daddy. He says everything, good and bad, comes from the holy hands of God.

Daddy laughs while little Mary and I help cover his hurts at home. Well while I try to cover them. Little Mary's too busy making him laugh by spinning around in the white cloth I'm stretching around his head. Her spinning twists my insides like the cloth until I explode.

"How can you laugh after that man did this to you?!"

I use two end marks for that sentence. What would teacher call that? She'd probably just shake her head like Daddy shakes his before he lets it fall heavy into his hands. It hangs there for a long time before his eyes find and freeze me inside of them as he says, "God never forsakes us, and we must do the same for Him. His image is in everything that happens. Everything except for the fags. God did not make the fags. God made men, and they chose to turn their backs on him and towards sinful fornication with their fellow man."

"But we need to use more than our signs and songs! We need to hurt them like they hurt you, so they will listen." I see my reflection stand strong in his eyes.

"The fags stand as a testament to how we will not be. They are in violation of the word of God and violent in the defense of their sins. We will not be."

"But they hurt you!" I lose myself in his eyes as they harden.

"And God will hurt them. God will unleash his wrath upon them when he sees fit. Until then, I'm not really hurt. My body may bleed, but the only part of me that gets to meet our God is stronger than ever. Remember that. You have a soul that no one but God can touch, and He will protect it always, just as I protect you."

His words wrap around me warm, like his arms. But even warmer is the hate that's wrapping itself around my heart. It wants to bleed.

It takes the same time for Daddy to heal enough to hold up a sign as it did for God to make the world. Once he heals, we all load up in the van and head to Rochester Cemetery where sins are being buried.

Because the people with the power in this country are fag-lovers, we are only allowed as close as across the street. That just means we sing our songs extra strong, so they are heard by all the people at the fag-lover's funeral. For most of the time, the fag-lover's family acts like it can't see our signs or hear our songs, and I feel anger sizzle under my skin like the hot stove when Mom spills on it. At most funerals, it's the fags and those who love them whose faces are mad masks while I laugh. I don't laugh today. Instead, I wait until the waves of people wash towards their cars, and then I sing my favorite song:

First to fight for the fags,
Now you're coming home in bags,
And your army goes marching to hell.
Proud of all of your sin,
No more battles you will win,
And your army goes marching to hell.

Then it's IEDs,
Your army's on its knees,
Count off the body parts all gone (Two! Three!)
And where e'er they go,
The dying soldiers show,
That your army keeps marching to hell!

The faces of the fag-lover's family look like the characters in my comic books when I fan through them really fast. Each line turns their faces into a new scene of pain. I smile. And smile. And then my smile slips. It slips off my face just like the tears slip down the face of a man sitting on the curb across from me. I feel them like they're dripping onto me and drowning me drop by drop. I struggle to breathe as he says, "That's my brother you're talking about. The bravest man I . . ." Tears take over his voice, and anger at the lie he just told takes over me. God is not sad for liars or fags, and I will not feel sad for this man who loves both.

"He died because God hated him, and you should be happy he's in hell!"

And I can breathe again. I breathe in the sharp smell of Gramps's tobacco that hugs his shirt as he hugs me.

"My boy, you make me and God proud."

I wear Gramps's words like a medal all the way home. I didn't know he felt the way about me that I feel about him when I sneak into his study. That's where I stare at my reflection in the shiny of all his awards for something called civil rights. I'm not entirely sure what that means, but I do know that Gramps was one of the only people in the state who would defend black people before they were treated like people. It got him lots of honors, but a lot more hate. Samuel says that the phone rang so much with scary sentences on the other line, Gramps pulled it out of the wall. He didn't throw it, though. The way those angry people threw rocks through the windows. Were their words sharper or the glass? I think the words were.

Words are the most powerful things in this world. Gramps taught me that. God made this entire world with words alone. We can create with words too. With words we can plug into other people and light them up with love. Sometimes it takes a while, like the dusty lamp that hangs over Gramps's desk, but once he plugs it in, it always works. If light cords didn't have the pokey ends they do, they couldn't stick into light sockets and make light. Sometimes you need sharp words to sink into people and reach their souls. We use the sharp words we do because we love God's people, and we want our words to stick inside them so that they stop sinning. We love them, and we want to save them. Sometimes love looks a lot like hate. It heats you up, steals your head, makes your heart work extra hard. It makes you do things with your whole soul.

I try to tell Mary this a few days after the funeral when we go back to the cemetery with sidewalk chalk. Mary just keeps quietly coloring her Bible verse, but when she finishes she mumbles to it, "The words we say to people don't make them shiny. They make us shiny. But they make most people red. Angry red or crying red. And then they hurt us and make us red."

She hands me her yellow chalk, and I give her my red. She uses it to draw the outline of a heart. I turn away and walk into the cemetery, thinking. Gramps tried to help people by being nice and it won him a lot of shiny awards, but the hateful people kept sinning and sending rocks through the windows. They broke just like Daddy's skin when the cinnamon-bear man attacked him. But he told me we don't hurt the sinners like they hurt us. We love them and that's why we use our sharp words. They might make us bleed, but with our sharp words we will make them see the truth so that . . . the sound of soft crying is suddenly louder than my thoughts.

Looking around, it takes me a long time to find the man they're coming from because he's slumped over to the same size as the tombstone he's kneeling by. I can't be for sure, but it looks like the same place fag-lovers were burying that sinful soldier the other day, and the sad slump of the man looks the same. I hide behind another tombstone and watch him. I'm close enough to see that his face is red from tears. His face isn't the same red as the faces of the kids at school or the face of the cinnamon-bear man. His face is red like Joanna's when she got hit by that car and red like Daddy after he was smashed under the cinnamon-bear man and red like Teacher's face when I tell her she's going to hell and the same red as the funeral people's faces when I sang my song. These thoughts shout the sameness of these shades of red louder than the sad-slumped man's crying, and I don't notice that he's stopped until he's gone.

I walk slowly over to the grave I wasn't allowed to stand by during the funeral. The grave of the brother of the sad-slumped man. I fit my knees into the little valleys the sad-slumped man's knees made and look at the tombstone. "Jonah," it says. The sad-slumped man's brother's name was Jonah. I want to leave something for him and something for the sad-slumped man to see when he comes back, but I don't have anything but my red chalk. I stare at how the chalk's made my hands all red, and it gives me an idea.

Real slow, I draw half a question mark like the mark you put at the end of a sentence you don't know the answer to, and then I draw another one to match and make a heart. I smile at the way two red question marks make a heart and then I stand up. The fresh dirt from Jonah's grave has grabbed onto the knees of my pants, but I leave it there as I leave the cemetery to find Mary. She's waiting for me by the gate, standing in a sea of yellow hearts she's drawn all over the sidewalk.

"Do you remember the soldier's funeral we sang at here?" I ask her this softly like if I talk too loud it will smear the chalk hearts, and she nods just as soft.

"His name was Jonah."

She smiles, grabs my red chalky hand with her yellow chalky one, and we walk back home careful not to step on any hearts.

JENSEN REED
I See Your Monsters

THE SOLDIER ROLLED HIS SHOULDERS as he stared at the rocky mountainside before him. His sword arm was sore and barely responsive, but he flexed and stretched it, trying to loosen the taut muscles. He needed to be prepared. He watched as a small segment of the mountain twitched, like a horse trying to rid itself of a fly.

"But why?" A small voice broke through the soldier's thoughts. He blinked several times, and suddenly he was back in a small, purple bedroom. He looked at the sleepy child in her bed at his side and reached over to stroke her cheek.

"Why what?" he asked softly.

"Why did the mountain move, Papa?" she asked before coughing hard. Her tiny body convulsed with each cough, and it took everything in him not to reach down, scoop her up, and rush her back to the hospital. He waited until she calmed and took a drink of the water he offered before speaking.

"Because it's alive, sweetheart. Let's keep reading, yeah?"

She nodded and pulled her purple blanket up to cover her thin arms. He picked up the book and opened the page again to show her the photo of a lone soldier who stood against a gargantuan mountain. He held a long silver sword in his right hand, and it pointed out towards the rolling grass at his side. The thick black cloak billowed around his legs as the breeze blew past and bent the tall grass all around him.

"He looks like you, Papa!" she said with a smile. He smiled down at her as he continued reading, knowing she would interrupt again. But if it prolonged their story, then he didn't care.

With a deep grumble, the mountain shifted slightly. The soldier widened his stance to keep his footing and waited.

"What's he waiting for, Papa?" she whispered.

"To face the monster, sweetheart."

"Oh. Why?" she asked again, and he closed the book, keeping his thumb on the page as he turned to look at his only child.

"Because it's his job to protect the people."

Her tiny brow furrowed as she thought about his words. "But what did the monster do?"

"I don't think this story tells us."

She continued to stare towards the wall, deep in thought. After a moment she looked up at him. "It's the soldier's job to fight the monsters?"

"Yeah." He smiled softly at her.

"But, not all monsters are ones you can see, right?"

He closed his eyes briefly before he nodded. "Yeah. That's right." His voice cracked with emotion as he cupped her head in his hand.

"Like the cancer," she added in a matter-of-fact tone. He nodded, unable to form words around the lump of emotion in his throat.

"So, can this soldier fight the cancer too, Papa?" she asked, peering up at him with owlish blue eyes.

He opened his mouth to tell her no, to say that cancer was something that they couldn't fight with swords and fists. But he also wanted to assure her that maybe there was still hope when everything else had failed. He wanted to say yes, so he wouldn't feel this crushing weight on his chest. He wanted to end this fear of leaving her side in case it was the last time.

"Can I sit with you, sweetheart?" he said instead. She nodded again and scooted over, making room for his large frame in her tiny twin-sized bed. The squishy mattress sank beneath his weight, and she fell easily against his side.

She settled her bare head on his bicep and one of her thin hands rested on his broad chest.

"I love you," he said as he wrapped his arm around her, so he could hold the book again.

"Love you too, Papa. Can we finish the story? I'm tired."

"Of course."

The soldier turned to look over his shoulder with bright blue eyes and a set jaw. He focused on a small child that sat huddled on the ground, staring back up at the tall soldier.

"Can you see it move, too?" the child asked in a trembling whisper. The soldier nodded.

"I see your monsters, child," he spoke in a gravelly voice, and when he did, the mountain began to writhe. "I'll chase them away," he added before turning back to the monster that was rising to its feet. Each claw was the height of the soldier, but he stood firmly rooted in his spot between the child and creature.

"Do you see the monster's eyes, sweetheart?" he asked, knowing she would like the catlike pupil. He reached up to brush his hand over her head, missing her red curls. "Are you asleep?" he whispered, glad she was finally able to. He set the book up and turned on the bed, the springs creaking under him.

Her eyes were closed as she rested against him. He smiled at her sweet face for a brief, peaceful moment. Then a thought started tugging at his mind, and he swallowed before shifting his gaze to her chest. The image of the cat on her shirt was still without her breath to move it.

He swallowed away the lump in his throat as he reached over to place his hand across her chest. There was no movement. His breath hitched as he looked at her peaceful face.

"Elly?" he asked in a broken whisper, knowing she wouldn't respond. "El?" he said again before he wound his arms around her and pulled her to his chest. Tears burned his eyes as his wife appeared in the doorway, her hair still wet from the shower. She froze, towel in her hand as she stared at them. He couldn't push words past his numb lips, so he just shook his head. With a strangled cry, his wife rushed to the bedside, the towel forgotten in the hall.

She ran her hands over Elly's bony back and head as sobs ripped free from her chest.

He closed his eyes and cradled his daughter as his wife crawled into the tiny bed too. It had been a long time coming, but he wasn't ready. He would never be ready. He wasn't strong enough for this. As tears rolled down his face, he heard his daughter's voice in his mind, comparing him to the strong soldier. He shook his head, knowing he had never stood a chance against her monsters.

ELIZABETH SEDERBURG
Attendance Optional

I REMEMBER HER EYES were closed. Her face was all scrunched up and her eyebrows were knitted together like she was concentrating on some impossible math problem. Parents around her were trying to take photos of their kids. The hipsters with their boyfriend jeans and yellow-tinted sunglasses were pulling out their Polaroid cameras, and two assholes were leaning over the railing, watching their spit turn into nothing as it hit the water below. She just stood there.

After a long time, she sighed and slowly walked back toward me. Her long, blonde tangles of hair whipped across her face, blowing wildly in the wind. The sun was haloing around her head, making her look like a sad, sad angel.

I asked her what was wrong.

She shrugged and said, "I don't know. I just thought it would be cooler. You know, like maybe I'd experience something profound—I don't really know."

"Yeah, okay, well I'd say that straddling the make-believe line between Iowa and Nebraska isn't really something quite *earth-shattering*."

She rolled her eyes at me and we walked over to sit on a bench. After ten minutes of silence that consisted of her brushing her fingers through her tangled mass of hair, she glanced at me and whispered, "Maybe we just have to shatter the earth ourselves."

She stood up on the bench and stretched her arms out as far as they would go like she was reaching for something too far away. I remember how she looked around at everyone, moving her eyes from side to side, sweeping up and down the long bridge. For a moment everything was quiet. And then she roared.

"HEY! HELLO! HOLA, FELLOW HUMAN BEINGS!!"

I didn't even know what to think right then.

"HAVEN'T YOU GUYS EVER JUST WANTED TO BE IN TWO PLACES AT ONCE?! OR LIKE, DO SOMETHING DIFFERENT—*FEEL* SOMETHING DIFFERENT?! GOD! IT'S ALL REALLY BULLSHIT, YOU KNOW THAT? THIS WHOLE DAMNED THING!"

By then, the parents had stopped trying to round up their kids, the hipsters already posted their Instagram photos, and the two assholes were farther off down the bridge giving spit showers to a different part of the river (don't they know it all goes to the same place?). Everyone was looking in our direction trying to look like they *weren't* looking in our direction. I laughed.

"Oh, fuck it . . . Fuck it!" I stood up on the bench with her and yelled at the people. I screamed at the birds and the clouds and at the voices in my head telling me this wasn't normal. I remember that moment seemed to last for an eternity because I didn't know what time was anymore. We were lost somewhere both inside and outside of ourselves.

NATHAN SOUSEK
The Prettiest Sound

THE ICE SLID FARTHER INTO the glass of sun tea, settling with all the pretentiousness of wind chimes in a soft breeze—a sound that Nana said was the most beautiful sound in the whole entire world.

Riley wasn't so sure.

For one, there were lots of pretty sounds in the world. Mrs. Parsons singing in the choir at Sunday church services; a summer rain on the roof as you lay in bed at night; birds chirping outside your window in the morning (right before you want to jump out of bed and wring their little beaks for not being asleep themselves); the solid *thwack* of a baseball into your glove when you catch the third out to win the game.

Or the way Colby Anderson enunciated her name when she'd pretend like she was upset at him. The way he'd act all hurt and try to get her attention by dragging out the 'rai' part nice and slow, scrunching his face up in an exaggerated pout so that his freckles dissolved away like cinnamon on butter toast. How, just when she thought she could make him whine awhile longer, he would go and flick that wonderful 'lee' sound at her with his silver tongue, the playfulness flashing back into those sparkling green eyes of his. *That* was a sound.

But ice melting down into a glass of sun tea? That didn't seem like one of them.

Even so, that's what Riley found herself pondering as she sat on her nana's porch, just like she had last Sunday afternoon—and every blue-sky, sun-shining, get-dirty, go-outside-have-fun Sunday afternoon before that—that she spent sitting on her nana's porch all summer. Sitting on her nana's porch. Staring down at the glass resting beside her. Listening and pondering about the sound of ice shuffling in sun tea.

"Mmmm."

Riley glanced to her left to see Nana sitting in her rocking chair. She had her eyes closed as she rested her head back against the headrest, her arms laid out upon the armrests. A smile of contentment creased across her full rosy lips, bringing warmth to her complexion only a grandmother of Nana's proportions could achieve. Nana was an ample woman, as Papa used to say.

"Enough woman to warm a man's bed and then some, but not so much she'd overrun his house," he'd chuckle to himself as he continued peeling the bucket of potatoes with which Nana had tasked him. Nana would always threaten to salt his sweet tea if he kept that nonsense up and would chase him out the door, but Riley knew on more than one occasion Nana would smile secretly to herself afterwards.

Looking how Nana sat within her rocking chair, Riley decided Papa had been right: Nana was an ample woman. She wore a navy-blue sundress tied at the waist with a wide lace belt and decorated with cream-colored lace frills about the neck and flounce—the perfect wrapping hiding endless hugs and kisses and the wise remarks. A small table sat past her where sat a large pear-shaped pitcher and Nana's own glass of tea. She pumped her right foot, still slipped into her good Sunday church flats, slowly rocking back and forth so that the rockers of her chair seemed to hum across the wooden floorboards.

If Nana had a sound, Riley thought, it would be that.

The sun poked beneath the porch roof, sending beams of light through the pitcher and glass. Riley watched as the refracted beams cut across Nana, turning her already honey-colored skin a brighter tint of gold and came to rest on the floorboards at her bare feet. Riley wriggled her toes in the shifting diamonds of amber that reminded her of the kaleidoscope her friend Margaret once showed her.

The wooden *whack* of a screen door against its frame echoed from up the street.

"You think Ol' Hank will fix that rusty bucket of his today?" Nana chuckled without opening her eyes.

Riley looked up from her toes and stared down the street to where Mr. William Burdock, or Ol' Hank as Nana called him, made his way to his 1956 Neptune-green Ford pickup parked outside his garage. He wore a green linen shirt beneath denim bibs, the ones with faded oil stains, off-color patches, and more jagged stitches than Frankenstein's monster, the ones with the right leg ripped at the knee from where Mr. Burdock caught himself on the front bumper, a rip Mrs. Burdock had yet to mend or had chosen not to.

"Wouldn't help if he did. Ol' Hank's been fixing something on that truck of his as long as I've been sitting here in my rocking chair. Just as soon as he finishes fixing one thing and gets ready to take that truck out onto the road, he finds something else he has to fix," Nana chuckled again, her smile growing even wider. "Heh heh, some people never change, dear. Some people never change."

Reaching the truck, Mr. Burdock rolled his sleeves up past his elbows, withdrew a hammer from the truck bed, and quickly slid himself beneath the truck's underside. Riley could hear Nana smile to herself even as Mr. Burdock began hammering. She wondered if Nana thought Mr. Burdock's hammering beneath his pickup was a pretty sound. She didn't have long to ponder, however, when a nasally voice arose from around the corner of the porch.

"I see Ol' Hank is at it again, isn't he? I tell you, Martha, if he ever gets that rundown truck of his running, this whole town ought to throw him his very own parade."

Ms. Ira Sween stopped halfway down the sidewalk that wrapped in front of the porch and alongside the house.

If there was a word to describe Ms. Sween, it was proper.

From her chestnut-colored hair to her black-heeled toes, not a hair could be found any place but where Ms. Sween placed it. A large burgundy sun hat adorned with faux pink poppies set perfectly atop her head, her chestnut hair, a color defying her age, spilling out in cascading curls to frame her round face. A strict regimen of lotions and wrinkle creams had erased the age lines from her face except at the corners of her sharp hazel eyes. The way she smiled always reminded Riley of a hawk spying sparrows from atop a lofty branch. Most peculiar, however, was the way her hook nose, even when looking down, seemed to be turned slightly upward.

Her matching burgundy dress with flower print and pink belt hung mesmerizingly still as she stood out front of the porch, a beige fabric bag in her right hand, an oddly wrapped bundle of brown paper held in the crook of her left. That unnerving smile creased across her glossy, ruby lips.

"In fact, I was just talking to Mary the other day about her husband and that old truck of—"

"I do wonder, Ira, is there one proper reason why you're coming from my backyard?" Nana had opened her eyes to stare hard at the woman smiling in the middle of her front walkway. Her rocking chair had stopped humming, its silence a sudden heaviness upon the porch.

"Why, of course!" Ms. Sween said, drawing the arm with the unknown bundle closer to her chest. "Honestly, Martha, whatever reason would I have to visit your backyard otherwise?" she remarked with the hint of a smirk as she readjusted the package. "I was just walking by and happened to notice how beautiful your magnolias were this year! I just had to have a closer look. You know I was just talking with Alice the other day about her secrets for raising those wonderful effervescent flower beds of hers. You know how she has such the green thumb for that sort of thing. Why Miss Riley Bishop, I didn't even notice you sitting there! Spending another summer with your grandmother, are you?"

Riley didn't have time to respond before Nana broke in. "What's in the package, Ira?"

"Oh, Martha, you are too suspicious. Why," Ms. Sween said, the hint of smugness returning to her face, "sweet old Walter Stevens said the same thing while I was over there not half hour ago. He was sharing some of his magnificent fresh garden produce and canning with me. Even insisted I take some of that glorious honey he jars," she said positively smug.

Riley noted how Ms. Sween had only nodded to the bag and not the package wrapped in brown paper, the one she so tenderly drew tighter against her chest.

"You know how sweet he is. It positively shocked me when he said how terse you were last week when he stopped by on his way to the post office! I, of course, defended you, my dear. We proper ladies must stick together, you know."

Nana's face twisted into a grimace as Ms. Sween finished. The sun had sunk completely below the roof of the porch now, casting jagged shadows across her face in a menacing visage. "Sweet Walter Stevens? *He* said that about me, huh?"

"Oh, don't take it so seriously, Martha dear," Ms. Sween said, batting away Nana's stare as if a child were scowling at her. "I'm sure he didn't mean any offense by it."

For several moments, Riley couldn't hear a single sound around her, as if the entire world had suddenly gone stone deaf while Nana and Ms. Sween measured one another. Then suddenly, Mr. Burdock's hammering from up the street reverberated into the tense afternoon air, followed by the soft clinking of ice to the left of Nana.

"Oh, I see you're enjoying some of that signature sun tea of yours. You know, when you brought it to Young Allister's birthday party the other week, everyone just simply went on about it. Some of them still do after all this time! You must tell me how you brew it. It would go so perfectly with my turkey salad sandwiches. Everyone says so."

Riley noticed the subtle flash of greed as Ms. Sween finished.

"Good evening, Ira," Nana said slowly resuming her rocking. "And next time you pass by, do let me know so I can prune you off a few blossoms to fragrant that home of yours. Archie did always believe nothing fills an empty home better than a few fresh cut magnolias."

When Nana had finished, Riley noted the glint of anger in Ms. Sween's smug eyes.

"Oh, I do suppose it is getting late, isn't it? Well I suppose I should be on my way home then. You have a wonderful evening, dears," she said with renewed composure, her nose swept upward as she turned to leave.

Riley watched as Ms. Sween slid down the sidewalk and out of sight. Slowly she realized, Mr. Burdock was still hammering under his truck.

"Mm hmm, you listen to your nana, dear. Some people never learn to mind their own business." Nana was rocking heavily, her foot pumping along as if she were working her sewing machine causing her chair to 'va-rump' against the wooden floor. "They'll work their entire lives spying in your backyard just to get a look at your magnolias." Nana had her eyes closed again. She shook her head like she had just taken a sip of some overly sweet tea. "And no matter how hard you try to teach them, some people will never change. Never change, you hear?"

Riley sat silently, hearing Nana's rocking slow as the sun sunk lower in the sky, turning the golden diamonds on the floor into orange blotches more shadow than light. Down the street Mr. Burdock cursed after banging his head as he crawled from under his rundown Ford. He slammed the hammer against the hood as he stormed toward his house holding the side of his head. Riley noted the tear in his right pant leg had grown.

The wooden whack of his screen door reverberated as he disappeared inside as the first of the evening's cicadas began their wailing song. And as she sat, hearing the hum of her nana's rocker against the floorboards, the warm breath of Nana smiling, and the soft shuffling of ice in sun tea, Riley listened to the prettiest sound in the whole world.

RYAN SOUSEK
Nothing

I MET BECKI IN MARCH, right in the middle of the "Becky-lemme-smash" fad. She had these long sun-sandy curls—the kind Rapunzel envied—and eyes soft and alight with the piercing gentle hue of a blue jay's crest. Her body was fit but showed she would devour a bag of potato chips if you left them out while Netflix was streaming a mid-2000's sitcom, one where the guy meets the girl, and they both hate each other until they love each other more.

We worked together, the night shift, stocking shelves in the middle of grocery aisle five just off Main Street and Who Cares Drive. That's all, we just worked together.

She would laugh at my jokes from time to time. Maybe she was just tired because I know she was; we both were, but maybe she found them funny too. And if I really got her going, she would hit those wonderful silent gasps, turn a slight red, and her hair would get all askew, falling before her face smooth as silk curtains in the breeze of an open window.

I would watch with my big goofy smile spread wide, quietly chuckling at my own joke, as she would raise her hand to brush away those sun-sandy curls from her face and place them back behind her ear. I'd catch myself in a trance and look away in a hurry. But, girls? They always know when you are staring. So, she called me out every now and again on what I had been looking at. In those moments, every cliché of beauty washed over me. I could say fallen angels from heaven, the first radiance of sunrises, or the bane of young Romeo were unsuited, but truthfully, I blame my lack of bravery. To her, my response always sounded, "Nothing." "Nothing," the haunting word to let any girl know she's encompassing your world, but also all too demeaning to fulfill the feeling you bear.

In late July, she took a teaching position at the college downtown and left immediately to begin job training. I was dazed by the news and droned the rest of the conversation, which now I fail to recall. I transferred to day shifts a few weeks later and spent most of my time at a register being lulled into boredom by strangers.

Then, just before Thanksgiving, I ran into her. I had called in an order to get overly greasy, fast food from the appropriately named food truck, Greaser's Grill. The Grill had the 50's malt shop feel including the food and style of post-World War II America with a modern twist.

Living only a few blocks away, I walked to pick up my food, and as I arrived, the streetlight caught those sun-sandy curls peeking out from beneath a knitwork hat. Becki had just gotten her food, smiling all along, and before she started on her way home, we managed a quick exchange of, "how are yous?" as she passed on by.

About a minute passed, and I was partway home with my bag of burgers when I heard someone cry out "help" quite sharp and quick. I stopped, my boots stood firm on the sidewalk and listened. Had I heard a cry or were the wind and my boyish fantasy getting the better of me? I heard nothing after. I spun around, hoping to see anything to tell me the truth, but I saw only the few remaining customers at the Grill ordering food and conversing. Surely, if there had been a cry for help, someone else had heard it as well. Yet, no one showed any sign of having heard such a cry. I resigned that I must have only heard the wind, but I listened intently all the way home without even the wind's howl breaking the silence.

Two weeks later, and it's earlier today. Becki came through my register, she kept her head down and hood up. Her sun-sandy curls were dull and frizzy. I couldn't see her eyes, but I imagined they had grown dark, and when I asked what was wrong, she said, "Nothing." This time I was sure I could not blame the wind for what I heard, and definitely not, "Nothing."

TRENT WALTERS
Sweet Mysteries of Life

AT SIX, BOBBY HAD ATTAINED investigative powers beyond mere mortals. He'd sniff down who stole the Fruit Loops better than a bloodhound. He'd read Sherlock Holmes and Encyclopedia Brown but found them lacking; they only pursued trivia: *Who stole this expensive diamond bauble?* or *Who murdered that non-genius nobody?* Bobby penetrated the heart of all human mysteries, inscribing the methodology and results into his Big Chief tablet.

Sure, he solved the Case of the Sobbing Neighbor Girl's Missing Kitten. She was so grateful she trailed him everywhere. He solved the Case of Why Joey's Beagle Howled at Night. He also solved the baffling Case of the Purloined Checkbook, which happened to be in Dad's coat pocket. His inhuman yell and throwing dirty clothes out of the hamper was curious since he'd put it in his coat an hour earlier.

No, these cases were nothing compared to the real questions that had to be addressed.

Bobby asked, *Is flesh composed of combustible material?* and found that, indeed, when sunlight focused through a magnifying lens upon the back of an ant, the carapace could be made to smoke.

He asked, *What flesh does a man need to survive?* and followed the lives of various grasshoppers, removing this appendage and that, or this antenna before that mandible and vice versa, tapping them with his fat pencil to watch the movement of the remaining parts, discounting reflexes and spasms where possible.

Foolishly, he shared his experiments with his best buddy, Joey, and his mother, who was making peanut butter and cheese sandwiches. She recoiled and dropped the half-sandwich peanut-butter side down, which Bobby notated in his Big Chief journal—an ongoing experiment.

Her reaction suggested she either didn't understand science or she was an alien, horrified that he was onto their alien secrets. He divided a page into two columns and scratched down headers for why she might be human and why not. He would need to test each assertion. He tapped his fat pencil eraser against his front teeth before ripping out the paper, crinkling it up, and slapping the tablet shut. She would be a lousy test subject since he could not keep her under observation at all times.

His penultimate inquiry had been to ask if animals bore souls. Using nothing more than his turtle aquarium, a two-compartment Plexiglas cage bored with holes to allow free movement of air, a candle, a matchbox, two heat lamps and his sister's gerbils, he turned off all but the two lamps shining at different angles, lit the candles and let them consume the oxygen under the aquarium. He waited with bated breath as each gerbil scrabbled and pawed at the Plexiglas of the upper compartment before the gerbils collapsed to their sides, panting. Once the chests ceased expansion, he watched for unusual stirrings of the candle smoke in all three dimensions—who knew the true direction of the well of souls except the souls themselves?—tallying the results. He mailed his conclusions to *Science* magazine and awaited their reply.

He refused to rest on laurels. The final experiment required much effort and planning, matching the pitch of his cough to the sound of the car lock. Once, his mother had caught him playing with the door lock, and he spent an entire car trip to Piggly Wiggly's feigning complete indifference to it.

His operative hypothesis was that aliens were observing his genius at work. No doubt his parents were in their employ, for how could two simple people give birth to so great a mind? Everything about him was a construct: the peculiar behavior of his parents (of course), Joey's pretended bafflement of Bobby's experiments to learn how the superior human mind functions, and even the reality of his surroundings. Why would aliens build a sprawling, elaborate TV stage involving props strewn across hundreds of miles when a handful of actors could play on only a handful of stages? Supporting his hypothesis was that many of the houses in his neighborhood resembled one another, showing a lack of human imagination. This pointed to the conclusion: either he had discovered a fatal flaw in the aliens' design or that the aliens waited for him to discover the obvious ramifications behind such a design.

And the settings that flashed past the car window? A three-dimensional image cast upon the window screen, giving the illusion of actual movement while the car stood still, gusting wind by the window with a huge fan, and adding a radio that played corny lovey-dovey soft rock on the back speakers to cover up the sounds of the machinery whirring in the background. Clever set-up but not clever enough.

On the day of the experiment, no clouds dimmed the clear blue summer and his keen observation. "Mother" drove him to the swimming pool. He coughed and unlocked the door. He checked Mother as she checked the rearview merely to watch for passing cops and cars on the Interstate. So far so good. He eased open the door handle . . .

The dashboard ding-dinged that a door was ajar. Bobby realized he'd neglected a vital step. Before his mother's confusion cleared and panic seized her that her experimental subject was about to escape and fathom the flaws of the experimental design, the door flew open as he pushed against the "wind." His mother screamed and slammed on the brakes. He leaped before the aliens had time to alter this consensus reality.

LIZ ZISKA
Bug Season

JIM HANNEN SKIMMED HIS NEWSPAPER at the dining room table while his wife was showering for the third time. The heat was brutal and *good Lord,* the bugs had become a near-biblical pestilence. People, even some in their neighborhood, were falling ill left and right. Some covered in mysterious bumps and bruises, some fatigued and bed-ridden. Others went delirious, streaking down the street at midnight, babbling about fairies and witchcraft. *Perhaps,* he thought, *the end of times is actually upon us.* He swatted at another no-see-um bug that swarmed and nipped about his brow. Never in his thirty-one years had he ever experienced such a nuisance.

There was a tiny, sharp pain above his right eyebrow that resulted in him slapping himself with the paper. His rimless glasses fell onto his lap, his left hand dumped over his cold, forgotten coffee. When he reached down to retrieve his glasses, the same sharp tingle plucked his finger. Suddenly, the no-see-um was not so invisible. He snatched up his glasses to get a closer look. He froze for a moment, then slowly started to reach for his rolled-up paper, trying not to startle the creature.

On his knee sat a miniscule woman, no bigger than his index finger, with purple skin and jet-black hair. She was draped in a tight bodice made of leaves and iridescent flower petals. The tiny figure rubbed her head and glared up into his ever-widening eyes. Then realization sat in.

"You can see me?!" she demanded.

Jim blinked once in response.

"Can you understand me?"

He blinked again. *WHACK!*

"What the *hell* was that for? It was just a question!"

Jim scrambled to his feet, brushing the pest off with the paper. "No. No, no, no, no, no, NO! Not me, I can't be sick. Quarterlies are due in two weeks, I am NOT dealing with this shit today!" He tried to stomp on the purple blur buzzing around his feet. In the next three heartbeats, his shoelaces were tied between the legs of the chair, and his advances on his assailant landed him on the floor, groaning in pain. Her wings buzzed as she hovered over his face.

"Listen, you great oaf. If you can see me and you can hear me, you need to calm the fuck down. I didn't mean to hurt you, so, please, stop trying to splatter me on the table," the tiny plea dripped with audible exhaustion.

Jim heaved a sigh as he clamored into a sitting position. "Alright. Fine. I'm insane . . . A mid-life crisis has to start sometime, right?" he muttered to himself.

"Quit bitching for one minute, would you? This is a bit bigger than one human's mid-life crisis. We little folk are trying to find all the humans that have descended from magical lines. A change is coming, and we need allies. Fast." She snapped her tiny fingers in front of his nose. "You still with me?"

Jim grunted, shook his head, and leaned forward to untangle his shoelaces. On his feet again, he tried to gather his wits about himself. He grabbed a towel and started mopping up the coffee-covered table and palmed the empty cup surreptitiously in his other hand.

"Good. You're calm. We're making progress. We haven't been able to convince anyone else that they weren't seeing things, so I'll take this much as a win . . . What do you know about mag—" *SMACK!* The empty coffee mug caught the wee woman unawares. Instantaneously, the cup began to rattle under his hand with a rapid succession of surprisingly hefty *thud-thud-thuds*.

Jim cussed under his breath as his wife rounded the corner from the hallway, toweling off her hair.

"Jim, dear Lord, what happened in here? You know the Johnsons will be here in twenty minutes for the cookout tonight! Have you even lit the grill yet?" Her eyes drifted to the cup pinned under his grasp, slightly shaking.

"Everything is fine, dear! I just knocked my coffee over trying to kill a bug. I'll have it cleaned up in a jiff. Would you be a doll and start the grill for me? I'll be out there in no time with the burgers." Jim tried to keep his expression as pleasant as possible, but that was becoming more difficult to do every second.

The mug under his hand had started glowing, vibrating faster and faster. His palm detected heat coming from inside it. His eyes swept between the cup and his wife's face in frantic succession. She shook her head and left to light the grill but not before the sound of shattering glass made her stop in her tracks.

"Dammit, Jim. What. The. Actual. Fuck?" His wife looked positively livid but seemed oblivious to the literally steaming purple blob that floated between them.

"Sorry, dear. I've got it. Go ahead. Everything's fine. Just fine," he managed to squeak out in a defeated tone.

"She can't see or hear me. She's completely non-magic. You, on the other hand, have a pretty strong bloodline. That much was clear when you could understand me." The tiny figure wiped coffee off of her leafy outfit.

"Nuh-uh. No such thing as magic."

"You can deny it all you want, *Jim*," the purple menace emphasized, "but magic is back. And we're going to need your help."

AUTHOR BIOGRAPHIES

ENERIS BERNARD-SANTOS is a junior at the University of Nebraska-Omaha, double majoring in Spanish and Creative Writing. Born and raised in Puerto Rico, she likes to incorporate fantastical elements and insights of her roots into her stories. She moved to Nebraska with her family to escape the financial crisis that plagued the island. In its stead, she found a steady home, a great education, and opportunities to experience a different culture and build life-long relationships. She currently resides in Bellevue, Nebraska.

KYARA BROWN is a military brat that claims Port Tobacco, Maryland, as her hometown. She completed her BS in English Writing at Wayne State College in Wayne, NE in May of 2018. She hopes to be a Contemporary YA Fiction novelist, have a library that even Belle would envy, and drink coffee on her screened-in porch every morning with her husband and pup.

TANA BUOY has lived in Nebraska all her life. After ten years of working in a salon, she decided to step away from behind the chair to pursue a new career, and in May of 2018 she completed her BS in English Writing at Wayne State. Tana is currently taking a year off to work on her novel and some other works before going back to school to obtain an MFA in fiction. She has works published in *The Flat Water Stirs, Judas Goat, Voices out of Nowhere,* and the *Norfolk Daily News: Literary Corner.* Her dream is to be a novelist, own a bookstore/coffee shop, and live in a beach house on Kiawah Island with lots of cats.

SOPHIE CLARK was born in Omaha, Nebraska, and is studying Creative Writing and Creative Nonfiction at the University of Nebraska at Omaha. She began writing as a songwriter at age fourteen and has since formed a local band with her triplet brothers called Clark & Company. The band has been playing for five years and has released three albums and one EP. Sophie is the lead singer and keyboardist. She hopes to further her studies in writing and is grateful to her family for their support.

GUSTAVO CRUZ is currently a graduate student enrolled in the Creative Nonfiction MFA program at Minnesota State University Mankato. He has a BA in English with a concentration in American Literature and a BFA in creative writing with a concentration in fiction writing from the University of Nebraska Omaha. Cruz comes from a family of military veterans and has lived at forty addresses in nine states. He has lived in Omaha, Nebraska for eight years and now calls Omaha home.

MOISÉS R. DELGADO is a senior at the University of Nebraska at Omaha double majoring in Psychology and Creative Writing (fiction). Currently, he is a copy editor for *13th Floor Magazine*. Moisés was born in San Jose, California, but grew up, and currently resides, in Omaha, Nebraska. Ask him the difference, and he'll tell you that California is orange and Omaha is blue. The former is family, but the latter is home.

A native of Omaha, Nebraska, **JIM FIELDS** earned his undergraduate degree at the University of Nebraska and his master's degree in English at the University of Nebraska at Omaha. After working his way through college in many fast food restaurants, Jim is an expert at making hot and crispy fries and rings. Currently, Jim is the Academic Specialist at Doane University. He is also an award-winning independent filmmaker.

KARA GALL grew up on a small family farm three miles south of Nebraska's Sausage Capital, Eustis. Her poetry appears in the award-winning anthology, *The Untidy Season: An Anthology of Nebraska Women Poets*, as well as *The Flat Water Stirs,* and *Bared: An Anthology on Bras and Breasts.* Her essays have appeared in the books *Women Who Eat, Why We Ride: Women Writers on the Horses in Their Lives,* and *Breeder: Stories from the New Generation of Mothers.* Learn more at karagall.com.

JᴀLEAH HEDRICK is a new writer currently located in Omaha, Nebraska. She was raised in rural Indiana, eating polluted catfish from the White River. She has poems featured in *Columbia Poetry Review, F(r)Online,* and *Manifest West.* In addition to writing poetry, she teaches in the Writing Center at Metropolitan Community College and has worked in Omaha's Old Market district as a professional baker.

JEN IPPENSEN is originally from Worms, Nebraska, and has spent many years living and working in small towns throughout the state. She earned a BA in theatre from Doane College, a MAEd in Curriculum and Instruction with an emphasis in English through the University of Nebraska-Kearney, and an MFA in creative writing through the University of Nebraska-Omaha. She was a Mari Sandoz Emerging Writer in 2018, and her work can be found in the Summer 2018 issue of *Midwestern Gothic*.

NICOLE KONECK-WILWERDING is a fiction writer who earned her MFA at Creighton University. She attended the University of Nebraska at Omaha for her BFA and has volunteered for the Backwaters Press, a nonprofit publisher in Omaha, Nebraska. She has been a semi-finalist in *N.Y.C. Midnight's* Short Story contest and was recently published by Tethered by Letters. She lives in Omaha, Nebraska, with her husband and two rescue dogs.

DAVE MAINELLI is a graduate of the University of Nebraska MFA program and has appeared in *Curbside Splendor* and *Fine Lines Creative Writing Journal*. He is from Omaha, Nebraska.

AMBER MAY was born and raised in the outskirts of Omaha, Nebraska. When she was younger, her grandparents lived in rural Nebraska on a three-acre plot of land. They lived right on the Platte River, and the author grew up fishing there. She grew up exploring the Nebraska plains and helping build her grandparents' house. Her other work can be found in *The Flat Water Stirs*.

DAVID McCLEERY works full time as a writer, musician, and landscape photographer in Lincoln, Nebraska. He is the former editor/publisher of A Slow Tempo Press, specializing in full-length books of poetry. David has published two chapbooks and has had his work published in numerous literary publications and anthologies. He is currently seeking representation for his first novel, *Grassland*. He is currently at work on a second novel and a collection of short stories. Learn more at www.davidmccleery.com.

JIM PLATH is an author of fiction and poetry. His work has appeared in *Inscape Magazine*, *Blue Monday Review*, *The Lowestoft Chronicle*, *The 3Elements Review*, *Amarillo Bay*, *The Monarch Review*, and *War, Literature & the Arts* among other journals. He holds a BFA in creative writing from the University of Nebraska at Omaha.

ELIZABETH POTTER is an emerging writer who has spent the entirety of her life in Nebraska. Deeply rooted in the fertile soil of the state, her work draws from this familiar landscape. However, inspired by the vastness of the Nebraska prairie, she seeks to extend her imagination beyond the boundaries of what is familiar into the uncomfortable and unknown places within the minds of the complex characters she seeks to understand psychologically through her prose.

A Nebraskan native, **JENSEN REED** grew up on a ranch in Holt County where her family ran a horse rescue. She is a writer by night after her days spent wrangling her two young sons. Married to her best friend and high school sweetheart, she's an all-around nerd who dabbles in numerous writing genres. Her current work in progress is an apocalyptic trilogy where she subjects her characters to the perils of a zombie outbreak.

ELIZABETH SEDERBURG is a college student from Elkhorn, Nebraska. Currently studying psychology, art, and possibly philosophy at Wayne State College, she dreams of living a life full of wonderful adventure on her never-ending search for the Great Unknown. One of her most important goals in this world is to help others see the magic and beauty that is often left unnoticed. Although quite ambitious, it is her hope to leave a positive impact on not only Nebraska but the world.

NATHAN SOUSEK currently resides in Wahoo, Nebraska, though he grew up the oldest of six on a family farm outside Prague, Nebraska. He graduated from the University of Nebraska Kearney where he earned his BA in Creative Writing in 2014. He has presented his work at several national literature conferences and most recently had several poems published within *The Flat Water Stirs: An Anthology of Emerging Nebraska Poets*.

RYAN SOUSEK, a Nebraskan native, spent his childhood roaming the creeks and pastures of his family's farmland with his brothers and sister. Ryan has always loved literature, nature, and creativity. He began writing after completing a poetry workshop during his sophomore year of college. His writing generally reflects on or relates to his life experiences and contains dark undertones. Ryan graduated from Wayne State College with a bachelor's degree in English literature and writing.

TRENT WALTERS lived in Nebraska for a decade, mostly in Omaha, but also in central and western Nebraska. He has also lived in Mexico and Honduras. Stories of his have appeared in *Pindeldyboz*, *Lamination Colony*, and *Penumbra*, among others.

LIZ ZISKA recently graduated from WSC with her MSE in English Instruction and Curriculum, while working as a graduate assistant and a part-time gas station attendant on the weekends. She is a Nebraskan writer, born and raised, who dabbles in every writing genre she can get her hands on. She is the youngest of four siblings, the aunt of eight beautiful children, and the favorite (albeit, only) daughter of her two loving parents. She aspires to become a professor of creative writing in the near future with not-so-distant dreams of owning a bookstore.